I0537412

THE GEMINI RISING ROCKIN' MACHINE

DOUBLE PLAY OF HUMANITY'S DISHARMONY

Double Play Of Humanity's Disharmony
Featuring Books:
Book Eighteen: Rock Or Bust
Book Nineteen: Fucked Up
Featuring The Lyrical Stories:
The Gemini One Suite Trilogy
Live Free For The Day - Live Free 'Til You Die (In 11 Parts)
My Life Is Not So Great (In 8 Parts)

Copyright 2016 by The Gemini Rising Rockin' Machine
ISBN-13: 978-0692724071 (Gemini Rising Rockin'
Machine, The)
ISBN-10: 0692724079

The characters and events described in this book are fictional. Any resemblance between the characters and any person including their names, living or dead, is purely coincidental.

Because of the mature themes presented within, reader discretion is advised.

For questions, comments you may send correspondence to. thegeminirisingrockinmachine@twc.com.

Official Website
www.thegeminirisingrockinmachine.com

The Invention Of Mind Rockin'

I've always been a fan of music, classic rock, rock and roll, hard rock and heavy metal. I've also always been a fan of movies, comedy drama, action, suspense, fantasy and horror. As a kid my hobby was writing lyrics that I created in my mind. In 2013 I took my hobby, my passion for music and movies and with them I created Mind Rockin'. By doing so I made myself become something that I never thought or dreamed of doing before and that was to become a self-published author.

My creation of Mind Rockin' works like this. I sit down in front of my computer and come up with a melody or score in my mind to go along with the original songs or lyrical stories that I am creating. However when you the reader/singer reads or sings the song or lyrical story, there is no right or wrong for the melody or score that you come up with in your minds, be it rock and roll, pop, country or rap. Mind Rockin' is a concept I created for persons just like myself, those of us that would like to be able to do or create something like stories or songs but with no opportunity knocking at the door this dream of ours stays that, a dream. Mind Rockin' is the only thing in the world where the person you are has the chance to use what's inside you instead of the usual way, where it is only one way for everybody, and that is the way the creator intended for it to be foretold or heard.

I'd like to dedicate this book and thank my Wife of Twenty-Four years, I love you Christina thank you for your Love and Support.

I'd like to thank all my Family and all my Friends. Thank you to all my Fans, I am a Fan of yours as well, together We can make a difference. Let's Shout It Out And Speak As One.

The Gemini Rising Rockin' Machine.

Discography: Books 1 Through 19 Song Listing
(Example) **Rock Or Bust**
341. = Book Numbering / **730.** = Original Numbering

Book One: Who Am I? – **1-20**

Book Two: Mind Rockin' – **21-40**

Book Three: Big Time Love – **41-60**
Book Four: Love High – **61-80**

Book Five: Siphon Your Minds – **81-100**

Book Six: Do You Remember Rock And Roll – **101-120**
Book Seven: Rock And Roll Bachelor – **121-140**

Book Eight: The End – **141-160**

Book Nine: Sunshine Dealer – **161-180**
Book Ten: Thunder Love – **181-200**

**Book Zero: The 2.0 Versions Of
Who Am I? & Mind Rockin'
(13 New 2.0 Songs)**

Book Eleven: Dog Day Apple Pie – **201-220**
Book Twelve: The Pig People Are Back – **221-240**

Book Thirteen: Gemini Dance – **241-260**
Book Fourteen: Gemini Beast – **261-280**

(Triple Play Of Love, Sadness And Sexy Lust)
Book Fifteenth: Pink Hearts – **281-300**
Book Sixteen: Sexual Amnesia – **301-320**
Book Seventeen: Party In Your Panties – **321-340**

(Double Play Of Humanity's Disharmony)
Book Eighteen: Rock Or Bust – **341-360**
Book Nineteen: Fucked Up – **361-380**

Book Eighteen: Rock Or Bust (Pages 4-33)

(Side One)
341. Rock Or Bust (730.)
-----. What Can I Do Now (Walls) (802.) (Bonus)
342. Inside I'm Freezing (683.)
343. Turned Off (682.)
344. Me Me Me (A Parody) (675.)
345. Mental Slave (603.)

(Side Two)
346. Time Traveling Is Not Cheap
-----. (Humping Back In Time) (503.)
347. Tirus X (Earth) (596.)
348. Yeah, If You Think (501.)
349. This Dark Place (466.)
350. The Devil Knows My Name (455.)

(Side Three)
351. Your Whys And Hows (Psychic Abilities) (392.)
352. Plug Me In I'm Ready (390.)
353. What A Damn Fool I Was (389.)
354. All The Dying (368.)
355. The New Frankenstein (363.)

(Side Four)
356. Grabbed In The Night (358.)
357. With And Within Myself (289.)
358. We Travel On (237.)
359. Unreal (187.)
360. Pain (141.)

(Bonus Songs)
Your Extinction (34.)
You Will Burn (25.)
God, The Devil And The Weed Smoker (In Six Parts) (847.)
Inhale / Short / Tomorrow / Smoking / Rainbow / Happy

Web Site Extras: **(Pages 34-47)**
Short Story #1: Tirg and Seralena **(Pages 48-53)**

341. Rock Or Bust

Get-Up – Get-Downsized
World – Eats-The-Weak
Big-People – With-Big-Money
Own the World – Everyday

Scraps – What-We're-Fed
Our-Tomorrow – Never-Comes
If-We Put – Our-Heads – Down in Shame
Blaming-Ourselves – For-Their-Misdeeds

(Chorus)
Rock Or Bust
Get Moving Or Get Dead
Rock Or Bust
Freedom Is Worth Some Of Your Time
Rock Or Bust
Let's Take Away Their Big Greedy Power

Suffocated by Power – From-The-Man
Manipulated in Believing in Them
Don't-You-Smell – Their-Stench
Do-They – Even-Wipe
When-They-Do – Wipe – It's-On-Us

Can-We-Blame-Them – For-Being-The-Man
It's-Our-Votes – That-Keeps
Fattening-Them-Up – So-Huge

Maybe-We-Should – Make-Them-Eat
What-We-Are – Forced to Eat
Sit-Back – Watch-Them – Choke
On-What – They-Can't – Stomach

(Chorus)
Rock Or Bust
Get Moving Or Get Dead
Rock Or Bust
Freedom Is Worth Some Of Your Time
Rock Or Bust
Let's Take Away Their Big Greedy Power

What Can I Do Now (Walls)

I-Walk-Wrong – They-Walk-Correct
Smile-On-My-Face – Tell-Me-This
I'm-Doing – Something-Yesterday
When the Sun – Shined-Down – On-Me
Just-Like it Did – On-All – The-Good-People
Those-That-Walked – With-Many – Bad-Habits
Odysseying – Themselves to Enlightenment

(Chorus)
What Can I Do Now
Walls – Walls – Everywhere
What Can I Do Now
When Everything Is Wrong
And Nothing Is Correct
What Can I Do Now
Walls – Walls – Everywhere
What Can I Do Now
Am I Even Allowed – Not To Like
Wiping My Own Ass

I-Walk-Wrong – They-Walk-Correct
Smile-On-My-Face – Tell-Me-This
Love and Hate – Inside-Me-Always
My-Constant – Fire and Ice

Their-Hate – Consumes-The-World
Love is Dead – In-Their-Hearts
What's the Sense of Hating – If-You're
Not-Searching for Love
That-Will – Take-Over-The-World

(Chorus)
What Can I Do Now
Walls – Walls – Everywhere
What Can I Do Now
When Everything Is Wrong
And Nothing Is Correct
What Can I Do Now
Walls – Walls – Everywhere
What Can I Do Now
Am I Even Allowed – Not To Like
Wiping My Own Ass

342. Inside I'm Freezing

World is Turning and Burning
Everyday – There-Is a Spark of Life
For-All – The-Sinners – Not to Comprehend
Inside-I-Feel – No-Evil / Inside-I-Feel – No-Good
Is-That a Knocking at My-Door
Is-That-Knocking – Inside-My-Head
I-Can-Never-Tell – They-Are so Alike – and
I-Don't -Feel-Like – Moving to Find-Out

(Chorus)
Inside I'm Freezing
With Out Love In My Life
Inside I'm Freezing
Knowing – I'd Rather Be Alone

Inside I'm Freezing
Am I Still Even – Alive
Inside I'm Freezing
I Don't Want To Feed The Clay
Until I Have Lived – Free For One Day

Cold – Empty – Lonely – Mind of Mine
Do-You-Even – Care-About-Life
Stand-Up – Stare at The-Sky
The-World is Not – Yours to Own
You're-Just – One-Lonely-Man
That-Needs to Survive-The-Life
You-Live – Until-Your-Dying-Day
When-This-Comes to Life
It-Will-Make-Me-Say – I'm-Not-Freezing

(Chorus)
Inside I'm Freezing
With Out Love In My Life
Inside I'm Freezing
Knowing – I'd Rather Be Alone

Inside I'm Freezing
Am I Still Even – Alive
Inside I'm Freezing
I Don't Want To Feed The Clay
Until I Have Lived – Free For One Day
7

343. Turned Off

World-Sucks – Not-In a Good-Way
Doom-From-The-Damned – Have-Entered – My-Mind
I-Want to Love – I-Want to Live – We-Seems-Not-To

Whose – Fault is This – I-Don't-Think – It's-Mine
Can-I – Blame-The-World – Can-It – Even be Blamed
I-Don't-Think-So – I-Don't-Feel-So – At-This-Time

(Chorus)
I'm Just – Turned Off
Can't Care Too Much
It Is What It Is
Blood On The Moon
Blood Under The Sun
Sex With Immense Hate
With No Cherry On Top
To Start The Meal Off – Just Right

Fake-Helps – Fake-Saves
Junkies-Jamming it In – So-Deep
Politicians – Our-Friends – They
Help-Us-Out – When-They-Can
Lonely is The-World – Lonely as My-Life

I-Think-About-Hate – It's-Boring
Maybe-So-Am-I – Don't-Care
What-Can-Be-Done – With-Boring and Lonely
Can-We – Un-Recreate – Fear and Hate
I-Don't-Think so – We-Has-Never-Tried
We-Has-Left – Without-Saying – Goodbye
Leaving-I – Once-Again – Bored and Lonely

(Chorus)
I'm Just – Turned Off
Can't Care Too Much
It Is What It Is
Blood On The Moon
Blood Under The Sun
Sex With Immense Hate
With No Cherry On Top
To Start The Meal Off – Just Right

8

344. Me Me Me (A Parody)

I-Take and I-Take
I-Don't-Give a Fair-Sake
If-I – Bring-You-Down
All-The-Way – To-The-Ground

Because-That's – Where-You
Belong – When-I'm-Around
I'm-The-One – In a Million
You're a Dime a Dozen

(Chorus)
Me Me Me – Me Me Me
It's All About – Me
Don't Get In My Way
'Cause Every Thing Is Mine
Me Me Me – Me Me Me
It's All About – Me

Go-Ahead – Complain-About
Everything – I-Have and You-Want
I'll-Turn-Around – Let-You-Talk
To-My-Complaint – Department

Even-My-Ass – Is-Worth-More
Then-Your – Doing-Without-Face
I-Laugh – All-The-Way to The-Bank
While-You – Reach-Out – For-My-Scraps
That-I'd-Rather – Throw-Away

(Chorus)
Me Me Me – Me Me Me
It's All About – Me
Don't Get In My Way
'Cause Every Thing Is Mine
Me Me Me – Me Me Me
It's All About – Me

(This-Song is designed to make you think and feel what a very,
very Rich-Person perhaps thinks and feels about the rest of us.
(Is this a Parody or is it the Truth? That is up to You to decide.)

345. Mental Slave

Time to Get-Up – We-Are-Glad
That-You – Are-Alive-Today
Hurry-Hurry – Don't be Late
Today-You-Must – Work-Hard
If-You – Want to Stay
In-Our – Good-Graces

We-Have to Honestly – Say to You
You-Are-Just – One-In-Millions
Matter – Not at All – Laughable in Fact
That-You-Think – You-Matter to Us
Only-Reality of Matter – Is-Your-Vote

(Chorus)
Don't Be A Fool – Mental Slave
Your Singular Thinking
Will Get You Nowhere With Us
We Control You And Your Everything
You Are Nothing But A Mental Slave

Why-Are-You – Trying to Run-Away
You-Fool – We-Can – See-You
We-Are-Watching – Very-Closely
Where-Are-You – Running to
Stop-Your – Foolishness-Now
Maybe – We-Can – Be-Civil

But-Don't – Count on It
Your-Singular – Thinking and Doing
Is-Costing a Lot of Money
That-You – Are-Not-Worth
Stop-Right-Now – Before-You-Become
Worthless and No-Longer – Needed

(Chorus)
Don't Be A Fool – Mental Slave
Your Singular Thinking
Will Get You Nowhere With Us
We Control You And Your Everything
You Are Nothing But A Mental Slave

346. Time Traveling Is Not Cheap (Humping Back In Time)

Looking-For a Good-Time
Wanting-Something – Real-Nice
Just-Pop-Yourself – Back in Time
Welcome-Back to The-Eighties
Where-You-Will – Have a Great-Time

Lovely-Looking – Big-Haired-Hotties
All-Tight – Pantsed-Up
Showing-Off – Everything-They-Have
That-They – Love to Show-Off
If-You – Are-Ready so Are-They
That-Will-Be – Very-Much-Money-First – Please

(Chorus)
If You Want It – You Can Have It
But You Have To Pay First
And Pay A Lot Because
Time Traveling Is Not Cheap

Don't-Have – Enough-Money
Get-The-Hell – Out of The-Way
We're a Fast-Paced – Company
We-Get-You – There on Time
Then-Bring-You-Back a Minute-Later
With a Big-Smile – On-Your-Face

Messing-With-Us – Very-Stupid
We'll-Leave-You – Back in Time
Taking-All – Your-Everything
Leaving-You – Back in Forever-Ago
Living-In a Cave – Searching-For-Fire
So be Willing and Able
Pay-Us and You-Will be Just-Fine
Having-Your – Quality-Time
Humping – Back – In – Time

(Chorus)
If You Want It – You Can Have It
But You Have To Pay First
And Pay A Lot Because
Time Traveling Is Not Cheap

11

347. Tirus X (Earth)

Our-Planet – Tirus X is Dying
Our-Sun – Junous is About to Explode
We've-Known-For-Years – We-Have a Plan
Death-Will be Dealt to Everything
Except-Our-Essence – That-Will-Remain – Forever

We-Will-Saturate – Tirus X – With-Our-DNA
Bring to Life – What-Does-Not – Live
For a Year or More – Tirus X
We-Make – Into a Brave-New-World
Too-Much-For-Us to Live-On-With
If-We – Weren't-Already-Dying

We-The-Elders of Tirus X – Live-Protected
From-The-Elements and Tirus X's – Citizens
We-The-Elders of Tirus X – Destroyed-Our-Gods
Becoming-Gods-Ourselves – We-Reign – We-Create

(Chorus)
Out Of Death – Tirus X
Exploding Into Space
We The Already Dead
Live On For Eternity
Deep Inside The Once
Dormant Planet – Earth

Tirus X's-Citizens – Partied to Their-Deaths
Sex and More-Sex – Like-Horny-Animals
Tirus X's-Citizens – Killed-Themselves – Out of Fear
Not-Having-It – In-Them to Live – 'Til-The-End of Time
Tirus X's-Citizens are Weak – We-Reign – We-Create

We-The-Elders of Tirus X – Tried-Our-Best
To be Great and Loving to Our-Citizens
They-Started-Wars – We-Ended-Them
They-Tried to Destroy – Tirus X – We-Destroyed-Them
They-Cried and Died – Very Bloodily – Everyday
We-The-Elders of Tirus X – Turned-Our-Backs to Them
Creating and Creating – New-Life on Tirus X

12

(Chorus)
Out Of Death – Tirus X
Exploding Into Space
We The Already Dead
Live On For Eternity
Deep Inside The Once
Dormant Planet – Earth

On a Beautiful – Summer-Day
Our-Sun – Junous-Explodes
One-Year – One-Year is All – We-Get
'Til-Tirus X – Explodes the Same
Burning-Death is Coming to Tirus X
This-Can-Not be Stopped – We-Do-Not – Even-Try
Creating-More-Life – Out of No-Life is What-We-Live-For

Last-Day of Life – On-Tirus X – Has-Come to Be
Tirus X – Has so Much-New-Life – Over-Populating-it
We-Die-Now – We-Will be Re-Created – Newly on Earth
Millions of Years-From-Now – After-Bring Her to Life – With a
(Bang!!! – Silence – Millions Years Later – Another-Bang)

(Chorus)
Out Of Death – Tirus X
Exploding Into Space
We The Already Dead
Live On For Eternity
Deep Inside The Once
Dormant Planet – Earth

Our-Planet – Tirus X is Dying
Our-Sun – Junous is About to Explode
We've-Known-For-Years – We-Have a Plan
Death-Will be Dealt to Everything
Except-Our-Essence – That-Will-Remain – Forever

We-Will-Saturate – Tirus X – With-Our-DNA
Bring to Life – What-Does-Not – Live
For a Year or More – Tirus X
We-Make – Into a Brave-New-World
Too-Much for Us to Live-On-With
If-We – Weren't-Already-Dying

(Repeat Chorus)
13

348. Yeah, If You Think

Pain-Rain-Blood – Hot-Burning-Concrete
Trash-Can-Breakfast – Quick-Puddle-Bath
Out to My-Office – The-Cold-Hard – Streets
At-Least-I-Don't-Ever – Pay-Any-Taxes – Ha,ha,ha

(Chorus)
I Got It All
Living For The Day
Is My Life Great
Yeah, If You Think
Living On The Streets Is Great

Fast-Taking-Lunch – Walking by Grabbing
As-They-Turn-Their-Head – Have to be Fed – Everyday
Don't-Have-Any-Money – Don't-Feel-Bad
When-I-Have to Take – Something
While-My-Hands – Are-Out
My-Thank-You's – Their-You're-Welcomes

(Chorus)
I Got It All
Living For The Day
Is My Life Great
Yeah, If You Think
Living On The Streets Is Great

I'm-The King of The-World
Got a Bed – For-The-Night
Lumpy as Hell – I-Don't-Care
Staring-At a Dirty-Ceiling
Not-Smog – Not-The-Moon and Stars
Morning-Comes – Gotta-Get-Up
Beds-Are for Sleeping – Not for Hiding – From-Life
I'm as Poor as Can-Be & I-Hate-It – A-Lot

(Chorus)
I Got It All
Living For The Day
Is My Life Great
Yeah, If You Think
Living On The Streets Is Great

349. This Dark Place

I'm-Alive – Inside a Small-Spaced-Pit
Carved-Out – Real-Ugly – Underground
I-Can't-See-Anything – But-Darkness
I-Can't-Hear-Anything – But-Silence
So-Far – There is Plenty of Air
To-Keep – Breathing-In

(Chorus)
Bugs And Spiders
Crawling On My Face
I'm Cold And All Alone
Can't Move Or Get Out Of
This Dark Place

So-Very-Hungry – I'm-Going to Catch
The-Very-Next-Thing – That-Crawls-By
Pick-Up-Something – Think-It's a Worm
Put-It – In-My-Mouth – It-Tries to Crawl-Out
As-My-Teeth – Sink-Down-Hard
Its-Thick-Guts – Slide-Right-Down – Making-Me
Sick and More-Hungry at The-Same-Time

(Chorus)
Bugs And Spiders
Crawling On My Face
I'm Cold And All Alone
Can't Move Or Get Out Of
This Dark Place

Plenty of Bugs to Eat – No-Water to Drink
Is-Taking its Toll – I'm-At a Loss of Why-This-Is
Happening to Me – Air-Flow is Slowing-Down
I'm-Being-Let-Known – That-I'll be Dying-Soon
Nothing to Do but Wait-For-It to Happen

(Chorus)
Bugs And Spiders – Crawling On My Face
I'm Cold And All Alone –Can't Move Or Get Out Of
This Dark Place
Bugs And Spiders – Crawling On My Face
I'm Cold And All Alone –Can't Move Or Get Out Of
This Dark Place

15

350. The Devil Knows My Name

Long-Time-Ago – Devil-Came-Around
Asking if I – Wanted to Sell-My-Soul
Devil-Had a Thick-Wallet – Offered a Lot of Green
Told-Him to Piss-Off – Go-Back to His-Hell
Devil-Smiled – Real-Nasty – Handing-Me-His-Card

I-Grew-Older – Sometimes – I'd-Take-Out
The-Devil's-Card – For-Consideration – Holding
It-Tightly – Thinking of All – I-Wanted
A-Better-Life – Feeding-The-World
A-Better-Life – Owning-The-World

(Chorus)
The Devil Knows My Name
And I Know How To Get A Hold Of Him
With One Phone Call – I Could Be
Living The Life Of My Dreams
Minus My Soul Of Course

Long-Time-Ago – Devil-Came-Around
Asking if I – Wanted to Sell-My-Soul
Devil-Had a Thick-Wallet – Offered a Lot of Green
Told-Him to Piss-Off – Go-Back to His-Hell
Devil-Smiled – Real-Nasty – Handing-Me-His-Card

One-Day – I-Picked-Up the Phone
Gave-The-Devil a Call – Got-Put on Hold
Listening to Some – Sad-Hell-Song
Thinking of Hanging-Up – When a Hell's
Receptionist – Came-Back on The-Line

I-Was-Told – It-Was a No-Go – Because
The-Devil – Don't-Pay for Something – He'll-Be
Getting-In a Few – Years-For-Free

(Chorus)
The Devil Knows My Name
And I Know How To Get A Hold Of Him
With One Phone Call – I Could Be
Living The Life Of My Dreams
Minus My Soul Of Course

351. Your Whys And Hows (Psychic Abilities)

I-Can't-Read – Your-Mind – But-I-Know – What's on It
You-Want to Know – My-Whys and Hows
Want to Know – Real-Bad – If-I-Have – Psychic-Abilities
Need-Some-Answers – You-Feel – Like-Your-Life
Is-Not-Yours-Anymore – Like-You're – Living-Inside a Person
That is Using – Your-Body – Doing-Things – You-Can't-Control

(Chorus)
Hello Come On In
Have Yourself A Seat
Let Me Look Into Your Eyes
Maybe I Can Help You
With Your Whys And Hows

You-Get – Your-Answers – Always a Toss-Up
Good and The Bad – They-Go – Hand and Hand
It's-What – You're-Willing to Do-With-Them – That-Matters
This is All-I-Can – Do for You – I-Can't-Live – Your-Life
You-Can't-Live – Your-Life – Wanting to Know – Every-Answer
Life-Is a Mystery – Where-We-Only – Get-Some of The-Answers

(Chorus)
Hello Come On In
Have Yourself A Seat
Let Me Look Into Your Eyes
Maybe I Can Help You
With Your Whys And Hows

You-Come-Begging – With-Your-Wallet – Wide-Open
Pleading for More-Answers – You're so Addicted
All-I-Can-Do – Is-Shake-My-Head at You – Saying-No-More
All-Your-Answers – I-Was -Allowed to Know
Given to You-Already – There is Truly – No-More
I-See in Your-Eyes – That-Fear-Has-Crept-Up – Making-You
A-Living-Being – With-Nothing but Doubt – Inside-You

(Chorus)
Hello Come On In
Have Yourself A Seat
Let Me Look Into Your Eyes
Maybe I Can Help You
With Your Whys And Hows

17

352. Plug Me In I'm Ready

You-Called-Out for Someone – Willing to Be-Brave
Willing to Take a Chance – Pave-The-Way – For-Everyone
No-Need to Look-Around – I'm-Your-Man – Yes-I-Am
I'm-Your-Dream – Come-True – Let's-Get-Started

Pain is Overwhelming – Don't-Mind – One-Bit – Feeling
My-New-Machinery – Working-Itself – Into-My-Brain
Hairs on My-Arms – Standing-Straight-Up – as
I-Think to Myself – What-Will-I – Become

(Chorus)
Plug Me In I'm Ready
No Time To Waste
Plug Me In I'm Ready
I Want To Be The First Person
That Has A Chip In Their Brain
Plug Me In I'm Ready
To Control The World

Laughing-Out-Loud – Wickedly to The-Ones – That-Try
Telling-Me – What to Do – Laughing-Even-Louder
Telling-Them the Way – It's-Going to Be – From-Now-On
They-Rise-Up-Quickly – It-Does-Them – No-Good

I-Control – All-The-Machines
I-Control – All-The-Machines – Around-The-World
I'm-Plugged-In – I'm-Plugged-Into-Everything
There is Nowhere – I-Can't-Surf – In-The-Data-Zone

Suffer – Mankind and Pray – Come to The-Reality
I'm the New-Man-Machine – The-New-God of This-Earth

(Chorus)
Plug Me In I'm Ready
No Time To Waste
Plug Me In I'm Ready
I Want To Be The First Person
That Has A Chip In Their Brain
Plug Me In I'm Ready
To Control The World

353. What A Damn Fool I Was

Being a Hero – Out of Nowhere – Is-Such a Positive-Rush
Just-Love – All-The-Love – I-Get-From-Everyone
Looking-Into-The-Eyes of The-One – I-Saved – Is-Worth-It
Alone – But the Hugs-After is The-Best-Part of All

(Chorus)
I Saved Your Life
Dying In The Process
What A Damn Fool I Was
For You Truly Suck As A Person
I Should Be The One Still Alive
Instead Of Rotting In The Ground

Getting-Hurt and Stitched-Up – It's-Part of Being a Hero
Having-Your-Blood-Spilled – Is-Not for Everyone's – Taste
Bruises and Pain – Gets a Little-Much – Putting-The-Faces
That-I-Saved – In-My-Mind – Makes-Me-Feel-Stronger

(Chorus)
I Saved Your Life
Dying In The Process
What A Damn Fool I Was
For You Truly Suck As A Person
I Should Be The One Still Alive
Instead Of Rotting In The Ground

Hurt-Myself-Bad – Last-Week – Walking-Tall – Is a Challenge
Put-On a Smile – Reached in Deep – Looked-Around
Man-I-Didn't-Know – Who-Just-Shot-Somebody
Ran in Front – Of a Car – Like a Good-Hero
I-Sprung – Pushing-Him – Out of The-Way to Safety
For-My-Reward – I-Got-Ran-Over and Squished

(Chorus)
I Saved Your Life
Dying In The Process
What A Damn Fool I Was
For You Truly Suck As A Person
I Should Be The One Still Alive
Instead Of Rotting In The Ground

19

354. All The Dying

My-Soul – Feels-Almost-Dead – Body is Scarred
This-Damn-Bloody-War – Is-Killing-Me-Slowly
Almost-Wish-Sometimes – That-I – Would-Finally-Get
A-Blade – Through-My-Heart – So-I-Can-Die and Kill – No-More

(Chorus)
War Was Created In The Bowels Of Hell
Blades – Shields And Blood
The Battlefield Is Battle Loud
You Can Hardly Hear – All The Dying

Silence in My-Mind – Entering-The-Battle
I'm-The-Assassin – Held-Back – Seeking-Out
Higher-Ups and Slicing-Out – Their-Guts
Targets-All-Dead – Fools – Guarding-The-Fallen
Attack-With-Rage – They-Are-Sliced – All-Fast and Nice

(Chorus)
War Was Created In The Bowels Of Hell
Blades – Shields And Blood
The Battlefield Is Battle Loud
You Can Hardly Hear – All The Dying

Being-The-Best-Assassin – Gets-You-Power
Gets-You-Gold – Gets-You-Wine and Woman
King-Treats-Me – Like a Hero – Would be
Star-Struck – If-I-Wasn't so Blood-Stained

Alone – Covered in Blood – Tears-Flow as I
Laugh-Loud-Heartily to The-Night-Sky
Redemption – For-My – Darkened-Soul
Tears-Wiped-Away – Stop-Laughing
Take-My-Sword and Wipe – All-The-Blood-Stains
Off of It – Readying-Myself – For-Tomorrow
So-My-Sword – Can be Stained by Blood – Once-Again

(Chorus)
War Was Created In The Bowels Of Hell
Blades – Shields And Blood
The Battlefield Is Battle Loud
You Can Hardly Hear – All The Dying

355. The New Frankenstein

War's-Been-Around – Before-I-Was-Born
War is Still-Around – Since-I-Died
War is The-Reason – I-Kill
I-Want to Live in Peace and Make-Love
Forever – Leaving-War – In-The-Past

Cut to Pieces – Still-I-Fight – Most of My
Limbs-Are-Useless – Like a Good-Soldier
I-Grab-One of My-Fallen – Comrade's-Limbs – Attach it
To-My-Torso – So-I-Can-Fight so I-Kill-Some-More

(Chorus)
Out Of Nowhere I Come
The Battle Field Will Never
Be The Same – Now That I
The New Frankenstein
Has Joined This Bloody War

I'm-Made – From-Dead-Humans
Just-One-Giant – Man of Meat
Kill and Eat – At the Same-Time
Enemy's-Flesh – Nourishes-My-Belly
Their-Torn-Off-Pieces – Heal-My-Body

King and Country-Men – Treat-Me-Like a Beast
Tie-Me-Up-Real-Tight – Scraps of Food to Eat
Which-Does-Nothing – For-Me at All

(Chorus)
Out Of Nowhere I Come
The Battle Field Will Never
Be The Same – Now That I
The New Frankenstein
Has Joined This Bloody War

Freedom – Breaking-My-Rusty-Chains
I-Am a Monster – Not a Beast
I-Can-Not-Talk – But-I-Can-Roar
Kill to Eat – Eat-Everyone-I-Kill
Will-Mankind-Ever – Leave-Me in Peace

(Repeat Chorus)
21

356. Grabbed In The Night

You-Hear of Monsters – Humans-Gone-Mad
Doing-All-Kinds of Hate and Death
Filling-The- World-Up – With-All its Evil
Everybody – Does-Their-Best – Not to Think – About-It
Believing-That-It – Will-Never-Happen to Them
I-Wish – I-Could – Say and Believe-The-Same

(Chorus)
Grabbed In The Night
Abducted By A Madman
Pleading Does No Good
He's Only Interested – In What's Inside Me
To Help Him Forever – Live Young And Strong

Out of Nowhere – He-Came – Nothing
I-Could-Do – I'm-Big – I'm-Strong – Still-I-Got
Grabbed in The-Night – Like it Was – Nothing to Him
Lying on This-Table – Watching-Him – Slice and Dice
He-Never – Talks to Me – Only-Into-His-Recorder
Screaming is Okay – Talking-Gets-Me – Punished

(Chorus)
Grabbed In The Night
Abducted By A Madman
Pleading Does No Good
He's Only Interested – In What's Inside Me
To Help Him Forever – Live Young And Strong

I-Take-The-Punishment – Hoping – He'll-Recognize-Me
As a Living-Human-Being – Full of Life
Every-Time – I-Only-Get – More-Pain
Crazy-With-Madness – I-Want to Cut-This-Madman
Apart – Telling-Him-This – Makes-Him-Laugh
Begging-Him – For a Fast-Death is Ludicrous
Soulless-His-Eyes – I-Will-Die – When-He-Wants-Me-To

(Chorus)
Grabbed In The Night
Abducted By A Madman
Pleading Does No Good
He's Only Interested – In What's Inside Me
To Help Him Forever – Live Young And Strong
22

357. With And Within Myself

All-My-Life – I-Believed
There-Is a God in Heaven
Not in My-Mind – But in My-Soul
Years-Have-Made-Me so Hard
Can't-Even-Think – Free-Anymore

God-Has-Become – Way-Too-Heavy
Monkey on My-Back – For-Me to Carry
So-With-Deep – Thought
It-Came to Me – To-Look-Out – For #1

(Chorus)
Out Of Survival And Freedom
I Cast God From Out Of My Soul
Leaving Myself – Feeling Peace
No More Feelings Of Heaviness – Now I
Live As One – With And Within Myself

Everyday – I-Feel-Blessed
For-There-May-Be – No-Tomorrow
I-Live-My-Days – Loving-Life
Like-There is No-Tomorrow

I-Let – All-The-Sad – People
Keep on Goding it Up – With-Their-Lives
While-I'm – Standing by With a Smile
Loving-That – I'm-Free of Mind – and
I-Don't-Ever – Have to Go-Back to Believing
That-I – Need a God in My-Soul

(Chorus)
Out Of Survival And Freedom
I Cast God From Out Of My Soul
Leaving Myself – Feeling Peace
No More Feelings Of Heaviness – Now I
Live As One – With And Within Myself

23

358. We Travel On

Dawn – We-Can't-Wait to Feel – The-Warmth of The-Sun
Last-Night – Was so Cold – Dark and Painful
It-Took-Away – Two-More of Us – They-Died
Silently in The-Night – Weak-From-Hunger and Sickness
Nothing-We-Could-Do but Let-Them-Go in Peace

We-March to The-Top – Of-The-Highest-Hill – Where-The-Sun is
Sitting on Top of Its-Peak – Our-Journey is Now-Over
Three-Maybe-Four – Fell to Their-Death's
On-The-Top – Of a Hill – Tears-Come to Our-Eyes
Destruction-Lies-Ahead – No-Life-Around – Everything is Dead

(Chorus)
We Travel On – Searching For A Home
We Will Tame This Land – America The Second
Brand New – Now That The War Has Ended
Leaving Nothing But Rubble – For Picking Through

We-Felt in Our-Hearts – This-Was-Going to Be-It
Finally-We – Find-Our-New-Paradise – Land-That
Not-Dead – So-We-Could – Grow-Our-Food
Living in Peace – With-Lots of Love-For-Life

Sight of Another – Hell on Earth – It's-Too-Much to Take
Many – Fall to Their-Knees and Cry to Death
Many – Leap to Death – Back-Down-The-Hill
Still-Standing – We-Catch – Our-Breaths
Down-We-Travel – Our-Hearts – Have-Turned to Stone

There is No-Tears in Our-Eyes – We-Are-The-Few
We-Are-The-Ones – Who Travel-On and On – Death
Is the Only-Thing –That-Can-Stop-Us – From-Traveling-On

(Chorus)
We Travel On – Searching For A Home
We Will Tame This Land – America The Second
Brand New – Now That The War Has Ended
Leaving Nothing But Rubble – For Picking Through

359. Unreal

Walking-The-Streets – Heading to The-Gutter
Drinking – My-Life-Away – Making-Myself
Feel-Better – Even-Though – My-Life is Crap
Got-This-Bottle to Help-Keep – My-Problems-Away
Keeping-Out-The-Real – So-I-Don't – Have to Deal
I'll-Leave-That-For-Tomorrow – When-I'm-Sober

(Chorus)
Today Is Another Day
So The Hell What
It's Just Like Yesterday
The Pain Is Still Too Clear
And All I Want Is Unreal

Had to Have a Simple – Surgery
Nothing to Worry-About – Doctor's-Done so Many
Awake and Waiting – No-One-Comes to Tell-Me
How it Went – Starting to Worry – Been-Three-Hours
When it Was-Only – Supposed to Take-One

(Chorus)
Today Is Another Day
So The Hell What
It's Just Like Yesterday
The Pain Is Still Too Clear
And All I Want Is Unreal

Finally – Doctor is Dragging – His-Feet – Tells-Me
There-Were-Complications – That-Were-Not-Expected
It-Was a Battle – Unfortunately-He-Lost and I-Died
Laid-There-Not-Listening as I-Was-Told
Doctor-Brought-Me – Back to Life – With-Death
Inside-Me – Now-I'm – Dead-Alive / Alive-Dead
I-Got-Up – Walked-Away – Then-Got-Very-Drunk

(Chorus)
Today Is Another Day
So The Hell What
It's Just Like Yesterday
The Pain Is Still Too Clear
And All I Want Is Unreal

360. Pain

I-Don't-Know if I – Want to Lose – My-Pain
It's-Been – With-Me – For so Long
I-May be Nothing – Without-It
Broken by Love – Don't-Want-Anything
To do With it Anymore – Love is Not-For-Me

Surviving – Quick-Moments with Others
Then – Back to My-Sanctuary – All-Alone

(Chorus)
Pain – Pain Is Me
Every Time I Open My Heart
More Pain Soaks In – And
Burns Itself Into My Soul
Pain – Pain Is Me
Every Single Painful Day

Pain-From-Keeping – Myself-Out-There
Just so Somebody – Might-Want-Me
Makes-No – Sense to Me
Nothing but More – Painful-Pain

I-Feel – The-Loneliness
Most-Times it's Overwhelming
Makes-Me-Lonely – Hurting in Pain
Always-Alone – All-Night-Long

Shame is That – My-Fantasies
Have-Become – Pain-For-Me as Well
Now-That-I-Realize – They're-Nothing but
Endless – Empty – Painful – Reminders
That-I-Have-Nothing – In-My-Life- At-All

(Chorus)
Pain – Pain Is Me
Every Time I Open My Heart
More Pain Soaks In – And
Burns Itself Into My Soul
Pain – Pain Is Me
Every Single Painful Day

(Bonus Song)

Your Extinction (34.)

As-You-Feared – The-Day-For-Your-End – Has-Come
No-Words or Thoughts – Will be Enough
Can't-Get-Yourself – Out of This-One
Wallowing – You've-Been-Nowhere
Sitting-By – With an Empty-Stare
Smelling-The-Sounds of Despair

(Chorus)
Now Your Extinction
Is Here To Take Your Life Away
You Are No Longer Part Of The Plot
Your Extinction Is Now Complete

Hands and Feet-Are-Cracking – While
You've-Been – Rotting-Away in Dismay
Your-Soul – Has-Been-Bled-Out
Nothing – You-Can-Do – As-Your-Eyes
Begin to Ooze-Out – From-Their-Sockets
Bones-Painfully – Turning to Dust

(Chorus)
Now Your Extinction
Is Here To Take Your Life Away
You Are No Longer Part Of The Plot
Your Extinction Is Now Complete

No-More – You-Will-Not be Ascending
Burned-Out – Erased-Like-Nothing
Not-Even a Blot of Texture is Left
Wasting – Your-Flesh is Melting
Mixing-Together – Bubbling-Away
All-That-Remains – Wind-Blows-Away

(Chorus)
Now Your Extinction
Is Here To Take Your Life Away
You Are No Longer Part Of The Plot
Your Extinction Is Now Complete

(Bonus Song)

You Will Burn (25.)

Come – Take a Look – See-The-Nothingness
That is My-Being – I-Am-Eternal – Ever-Lasting
I'm-The-Fear – The-Despair in All of You

One-Look and You-Will-Know – The-Ending
That-I-Bring is Not – The-One – Foretold by All
Your-Beliefs – None-The-Less – You-Will-Burn

(Chorus)
Burn – You Will Burn
Flesh And Soul Crisped
Nothing That You Can Do But Burn
So Accept Your Fate – Rejoice
Have A Nice And Wonderful Day
Because Soon You Will All Burn Away

I'm-Not a Devil – Guess-You – Could-Call-Me-That
I-Don't-Mind – Been-Around – Since-The-Beginning
Simple-Minded – With-Simple – Ideas and Plans
Never-Can-See-Me – For-What-I-Am

They-Keep-Me – God-Like – Out of Sight
To-Them – I'm-The-Opposite of Their-Almighty-One
He's-Salvation and Peace – I'm-Damnation and Pain

(Chorus)
Burn – You Will Burn
Flesh And Soul Crisped
Nothing That You Can Do But Burn
So Accept Your Fate – Rejoice
Have A Nice And Wonderful Day
Because Soon You Will All Burn Away

God-You-Think – That its His-Plan and Way
You'll-Be-Alright – Because-You-Believe
What-You-Don't-Understand – Is-That-Neither of Us-Exist

We're-Just-Thoughts – Put in Your-Minds
From a Long-Time-Ago – Created to Keep-The
Peasants in Line – What-Better-Way to Get to You
Telling-You – You-Will-Burn – Forever – After-You're-Dead

Unless-You – Do-What-They-Say – Obey-You-Can-Be-Saved
God-Needs – You to Pay – The-Church and Pay to The-State
Taxes is God's-Way – To-Get-His-Will – Through to You

(Chorus)
Burn – You Will Burn
Flesh And Soul Crisped
Nothing That You Can Do But Burn
So Accept Your Fate – Rejoice
Have A Nice And Wonderful Day
Because Soon You Will All Burn Away

Come – Take a Look – See-The-Nothingness
That is My-Being – I-Am-Eternal – Ever-Lasting
I'm-The-Fear – The-Despair in All of You

One-Look and You-Will-Know – The-Ending
That-I-Bring is Not – The-One – Foretold by All
Your-Beliefs – None-The-Less – You-Will-Burn

Someday-Soon – I-Will-Become-For-Real
Like-I-Said – I'm-In-All of You
One of You – Will-Start – Global-Genocide
On-This-Day – I-Will be More – Than-Thought
Or-Warning – I-Will-Finally be Born
From-All the Blood – Pouring-Out of You

(Chorus)
Burn – You Will Burn
Flesh And Soul Crisped
Nothing That You Can Do But Burn
So Accept Your Fate – Rejoice
Have A Nice And Wonderful Day
Because Soon You Will All Burn Away

29

God, The Devil And The Weed Smoker
(In Six Parts) (847.)
Inhale / Short / Tomorrow / Smoking / Rainbow / Happy

I. Inhale

The-Man – Smoked-Weed-Only-Once
Did-They-Inhale – Wouldn't-Make a Difference
Murders – Murdering-Around-The-Country
Still-The-Man – Wants to Punish-Those
That-Likes to Get – High on Weed

You-Damn-Sinners – God-Told-Me
Weed-Was-Created – For-The-World
What-Can-I-Say – God's a Toker
He's-Happy – Mankind-Improved-His-Weed
With-Tears in His-Eyes – He-Told-Me
Gemini – Spread-The-Word of Weed
Tell-Mankind to Stop – Killing in My-Name

(Chorus)
Man Don't Inhale
That Privilege Is For We
Not For You To Waste
Man Don't Inhale
Let We Have The Right
To Say – Yes Or No

II. Short

This is Going to Be-Short
For-I'm-Sad – And-Alone
This is Going to Be-Short
For-I-Feel – My-Soul is Dying
This is Going to Be-Short
For-I-See – Evil-Everywhere

This is Going to Be-Short
For-God – Has-Ran-Out of Weed
He's-About to Start – Drinking-Alcohol
This is Going to Be-Short
I-Feel-God – Might-Be a Mean-Drunk
This is Going to Be-Short
Heaven's-Turned – Cold-And-Silent
Hell is Bubbling-Up – Through-Earth

III. Tomorrow

Today is Not a Good-Day
Yesterday – Heaven-Came-Apart
Earth is Covered in Blood-And-Crap
Who's to Blame– God or The-Devil
Such a Damn-Shame – I'm-Almost-Out of Weed

Thoughts of Myself – Saving-The-World
Sends-Shivers of Doubt – Through-My-Mind
I'm-Just a Man – That-Smokes-Weed
That-God – Use to Talk to Sometimes

(Chorus)
Tomorrow Will Be My Day
God Sent Me A Fat Sack
All The Way Down From Heaven
To Share With Satan
Tomorrow Will Be My Day
I'm Gonna Get Fried Out With The Devil
And Watch Him Bogart My Heaven's Funk
Like The Evil Bogarter He Is

IV. Smoking

Rolling-And-Rolling – Joint-After-Joint
While-Satan is Destroying-The-Earth
My-Hands-Are-Shaking – Out of Control
I'm-Spilling – Weed on The-Ground

Heaven's-Weed – Better be The-Funk
'Cause-Satan is Killing – Everyone-In-Sight

31

Damn – I've-Lost-My-Buzz – Time to Do
Some-Toking – Before-I-Save-The-World
Damn – Satan-Looks-Evil as Hell
Better-Blow a Little – Smoke in His-Face

(Chorus)
I'm Smoking – I'm Smoking
Heaven's Weed With The Devil
I'm Smoking – I'm Smoking
Heaven's Weed With The Devil
Gonna Get The Evil One
Stoned Out Of His Mind

V. Rainbow

Alone-With-Satan – His-Evilness
Verses a Sack of Heaven's-Weed
Blood-Dripping – Off-His-Hand – Reaching-Out
To-Snag-Up-The-Joint – I-Pass-Him to Inhale
Amazed as He-Smokes it Down-To a Roach
With-One – Very-Long – Toke

Satan-Exhales – Coughs-And-Laughs
Watching as I – Fire-Up-Another-Joint
Reaching-Out to Take it Away – From-Me
Like-I'm a Nothing-More – Than-His-Supplier of
Precious-Heaven's-Heavenly – Sought-After-Weed
Satan's-Not-Enjoyed – Since-His-Exile-From-Heaven

(Chorus)
Rainbow In The Sky
I Love The Sight Of You
Rainbow In The Sky
You Look So Beautiful To My Red Eyes
Rainbow In The Sky
Praise The Heaven's – I Out Smoked The Devil

VI. Happy

Rainbow in The-Sky
Disappear – Before-My-Eyes
Heaven is Shining – Bright
God-Put-Down
His-Bottle of Demon-Alcohol
And-Picked-Back-Up – His-Pipe
And-Started – Toking-Away

(Chorus)
Happy – I'm So Happy
I've Saved The World
Like No Other Weed Smoker Has Before
Happy – I'm So Happy
I've Saved The World
Like No Other Weed Smoker Has Before

Satan's – Gone-Back to Hell
Earth is Free – From-His-Evilness
Finally – Mankind-Has
The-Right to Smoke-Weed
Happy – I'm So Happy
I-Out-Smoked – The-Devil

(Chorus)
Happy – I'm So Happy
I've Saved The World
Like No Other Weed Smoker Has Before
Happy – I'm So Happy
I've Saved The World
Like No Other Weed Smoker Has Before

Web Site Extras:
(Pages 34-47)

They Point And You Hate (57.)

Kentucky (In-Breds & Meth-Heads) (609.)

My Grave Won't Leave Me Alone (836.0)

The We In My Dreams (896.)

Stupid Human (You Are A Killer Now) (853.)

Don't Vote (872.)

Let's Have A Drink To 2016 (858.)

Famous Puppet (805.)

Love Beams (843. **A**) Gemini's Version

Love Beams (843. **B**) Starblue's Version

Oh' Weed (946.)

Don't Grope Me (998.)

They Point And You Hate (57.)
(Written ?/5/2013)

Souls of The-Damned
Have-Affected – The-Governments
Around-This – Blue-Planet

Time is Short – Time is Crucial
Open-Your-Eyes – See-Their-Evil
Before-They-Come-Up & Infect
Your-Mind-Body & Soul – With-Nothing
Besides-Doom & Gloom – That-Will-Make-You-Feel
Like-You-Have-No-Life or Soul – Worth-Having

(Chorus)
They Point And You Hate
It's So Easy For Them
They Point And You Hate
Can't You See The Evil In Their Eyes
They Point And You Hate
Like a Stupid Piece Of Brainless Crap

Souls of The-Damned
Have-Affected – The-Governments
Around-This – Blue-Planet

Time is Short – Time is Crucial
Open-Your-Eyes – See-Their-Evil
Before-They-Come-Up & Infect
Your-Mind-Body & Soul – With-Nothing
Besides-Doom & Gloom – That-Will-Make-You-Feel
Like-You-Have-No-Life or Soul – Worth-Having

(Chorus)
They Point And You Hate
It's So Easy For Them
They Point And You Hate
Can't You See The Evil In Their Eyes
They Point And You Hate
Like a Stupid Piece Of Brainless Crap

Kentucky (In-Breds & Meth-Heads) (609.) (A Spoof)
(Written: 09/27/2014)

Hee-Haw Y-All – Here's a Song – I-Wrotes
After-Meetin'-Me – Some-Good-People
Down on The-Farm
We-Crap in The-Fields
We-Eat a Lot of Hay
Milk – Our-Cows
Feed – Our-Chickens – And
Cook-Up a Whole-Bunch of Meth
Know-What – I'm-Saying

(Chorus)
Give-Me a K – E – N – T
Give-Me a U – C – K – Y
What's That Spell
Kentucky – Home Of The
In-Breds & Meth-Heads
And A Whole Bunch Of
God Loving – Pieces Of Crap
Know What I'm Saying

Out in The-Hills
We-Like to Do – Our-Cousins
Sometimes – Our-Sisters
We-Like to Keep-It – In-The-Family
That-Way – We-Can-Recognize
Ourselves – From-All-The-Sinners
Know-What – I'm-Saying

(Chorus)
Give-Me a K – E – N – T
Give-Me a U – C – K – Y
What's That Spell
Kentucky – Home Of The
In-Breds & Meth-Heads
And A Whole Bunch Of
God Loving – Pieces Of Crap
Know What I'm Saying

My Grave Won't Leave Me Alone (836.0) (Written 08-03-2015)

I-Feel-My-Grave – Calling-For-Me
Mr.-Death – Knows-My-Name
I-Can't-Run – I-Can't-Hide
Doom and Gloom are
Infecting – My-Madness
Is-There – No-Hope-For-Me

Sanity-Such a Long-Time-Ago
Days of Long – Gone-Past – When-My
Mirror – Didn't-Scream – In-My-Face
Are-The-Days – I-Want to Feel
Before – I-Start to Rot

(Chorus)
My Grave Won't Leave Me Alone
Don't Know Why This Is
My Grave Won't Leave Me Alone
Why Can't I Live My Life In Peace
My Grave Won't Leave Me Alone
Why Can't My Grave
Belong To Someone Else

I-Was-Alive – Yesterday
I'm-Still-Alive – Today
I-Don't-Know – About-Tomorrow
I-Feel-Like – My-Grave
Is-Trying to Trick-Me
Into-Joining – With-It-Too-Soon
Just so It – Doesn't-Feel-Lonely

I'm so Tired of My-Grave
Wish it Was-Flesh and Bones
At-Least-I-Would – Stand a Chance

(Chorus)
My Grave Won't Leave Me Alone
Don't Know Why This Is
My Grave Won't Leave Me Alone
Why Can't I Live My Life In Peace
My Grave Won't Leave Me Alone
Why Can't My Grave
Belong To Someone Else

37

The We In My Dreams (896.)
Written on (03/23/2016)

Deja-Vu – Every-Night
I-Dream – For a Moment
My-Dream-Self – My-Soul
Rises-Out of My – Mortal-Shell

Dreamers-Dreams – I-Enter
Dream-Food is What-I-Crave
Have to Become – Stronger
My-Dream-Twin is Evil
Waiting-For-Me to Die

(Chorus)
The We In My Dreams
Are Not The Same
One Is My Dream Twin
The Other Is A Stranger
The We In My Dreams
Brings Me The Power To Dream
From The Forever Pool Of Thoughts

Dream-Twin in Training
Evil-Stranger – Evil-Teacher
Dreamers-Do-Not – Stand a Chance
While-Bleeding and Dying
In-Their-Nightmares

Follow-My-We – Into-Dreams
They-Want-Me – To-Die
Watch-Them-Feast
They-Want-Me – To-Die
Watch-Them-Kill
While-I-Learn – While-I-Adapt

(Chorus)
The We In My Dreams
Are Not The Same
One Is My Dream Twin
The Other Is A Stranger
The We In My Dreams
Brings Me The Power To Dream
From The Forever Pool Of Thoughts
38

Around 1:00AM on 11-12-2015, I was getting ready to start on my rewriting of Purgatory's Full. The last few days have been going really good not great on the rewriting. Focusing has been my problem. Not on what to do but having too many ideas coming at my mind at once. My mind of late has been running on full and it has taken me a few days to find my center or my calm. So on the 12th I decided to write a new song first before I re-started on Purgatory's Full this night. I was in a great mood and ready to go, my plan was to write a love song or sexy song since I am on the new part of "Love Den". I've been turned on the last few nights before this night just letting this re-written part be as sexy as possible.

I closed my eyes and no love or sexy came to my mind instead I wrote this new song below. I thought to myself after I wrote this what a bummer, which changed my writing this night, I wasn't turned on, instead I felt a little hollow inside. Which changed my focus on the ending of the "Love Den". It was getting very close to the time for me to stop and go to bed the following afternoon so I stopped. I thought to myself, maybe I should put this new song below on my website that evening. I changed my mind and the following morning, on the 13th, I started back on "Love Den". I thought I would finish this time, unfortunately total focus was not mine so once again I did not finish this part but I did add some new material which needed to be added which probably would not have been added if I was totally focused.

Later that night my wife and I had our early evening together, dinner and talking, we took our showers, she reminded me it was Friday the 13th and asked me if I was interested in watching a horror movie. I said it sounded great, I sat down, turned on the TV and what was on the news was more horrifying than any horror movie we own. My wife by chance had not yet read this new song below, I let her read it and she shook her head and said it was too real to life. I told myself to forget it and not put this song up on my website. I've changed my mind, as you can tell, I'm not putting this new song up for shock value or for more hits on my website. Like many of you I'm confused and saddened that this carnage happened in France. This song came to me out of nowhere the day before this happened in France and I feel that I should share it. I may be wrong, I am not perfect and I do not know if this will do any good or harm. All I want, like most of you, is peace and love in a peaceful world and never to feel hate in my heart again.

Stupid Human (You Are A Killer Now) (853.)
(Written 11-12-2015)

Alone – In-Your-World
Such-Easy – Prey-For-Them
Very-Soon – You-Are-Their-Soldier
Taking-Out-Marks – In-The-Midnight-Hour

Fever-Dreams – Mixed-With-Emptiness
One by One – You-Are-Never-Done
No-Hope – No-Love – No-Contact
Just a Screen – Full of Faces and Numbers
That-Changes – Every-Day

(Chorus)
Stupid Human – Did You Kill
Because They Told You To
Stupid Human – Did You Kill
Because You Wanted To
Stupid Human – You Killed
You Are A Killer Now

Does-God – Hate-You
Because-You – Killed-His-Children
I-Do-Not-Know – We-Don't-Talk
What's-The-Difference – I'm-Stumped

Unless of Course – You're-Looking
For a Easy – Way-Out
A-Safety-Net – To-The-Stars
An-Afterlife – Security-Blanket
That-Allows-You – To-Enter-Heaven

(Chorus)
Stupid Human – Did You Kill
Because They Told You To
Stupid Human – Did You Kill
Because You Wanted To
Stupid Human – You Killed
You Are A Killer Now

Don't Vote (872.) (Written On 01/30/2016)
(Here is something for everyone
to think about before you Vote)

Time is Here – It-Is so Clear
World is Changing and Rearranging
Trying to Keep-Up – With-Humanity
That-Sins and Prays – Everyday

Happy-Faces – With-Big-Smiles
Will-Help – Save-The-Day
For-The-People – That-Don't-War
Yeah-Right – I'll-Believe-That
When-My-Ass – Learns to Sing

(Chorus)
Don't Vote – Don't Vote
Give-Them – Give-Them
No Votes To Tally
Don't Vote – Don't Vote
If You Vote – Nothing Will Change
It Will Just Become – The Same Again
Don't Vote – Don't Vote
If You Want This World To Change
Or You Can Press The Button – Like A Machine

Come-One – Come-All – Voting-Day is Here
Have to Save – The-Country-From-Itself
Don't-Talk – Don't-Eat – Don't-Fart
As a Matter of Fact – Do-Nothing – But-Vote
Do it For-God – Country and Yourself
Yeah-Right – I'll-Do-That
When-My-Mine – Switches-With-My-Ass

(Chorus)
Don't Vote – Don't Vote
Give-Them – Give-Them
No Votes To Tally
Don't Vote – Don't Vote
If You Vote – Nothing Will Change
It Will Just Become – The Same Again
Don't Vote – Don't Vote
If You Want This World To Change
Or You Can Press The Button – Like A Machine
41

Let's Have A Drink To 2016 (858.) (Written 12/30/2015)

2015 – What a Year
Kinda-Hard to Forget
That-Love is Still-Alive and Doing-Well
When-Every – Other-Day
Felt-Like – Just-Another – Bloody-Day

Sunshine – Does-Dry-Away – Bloodstains
That-We – Tried to Forget-About
But-I-Think – I-Have a Better-Idea
2015 is Gone – Fuck-It
2016 is Here – Let's-Not – Fuck-It-Up

(Chorus)
Let's Have A Drink To 2016
Let's Have A Drink
Because 2015 Fucking Sucked
Let's Have A Drink To 2016
Maybe We Can Do More Fucking
Instead Of More Fucking Killing

2015 – What a Year
I'm-Too-Dulled – To be Angry
What-Will – I-Not be Able – To-Say-In 2016
Does it Even – Fucking-Matter at All
When-I'm a Sin – For-Just-Being-Alive

You-Know – What-I-Say to That
Rock-And-Fucking-Roll
Because-I-Have a Better-Idea
2015 is Gone – Fuck-It
2016 is Here – Let's-Not – Fuck-It-Up

(Chorus)
Let's Have A Drink To 2016
Let's Have A Drink
Because 2015 Fucking Sucked
Let's Have A Drink To 2016
Maybe We Can Do More Fucking
Instead Of More Fucking Killing

Famous Puppet (805.) (Written 06/24/2015)

Do as They-Say – Yes-You-Do
You-Don't – Know-Any-Better
World-Has-Changed – Your-Thoughts
Is-Simply – Just-Shit in Your-Head
That-They-Command – You to
Keep to Yourself – At-All-Times

I'm-Free – I-Own-Myself
Frowning as I-Laugh – Looking at You
Can't-Believe – I-Have to Say-This
To a World – That is Not-Listening

(Chorus)
Famous Puppet – Famous Puppet
Look At You Over There
With Your Skin Hanging Off
Like You Mean a Fucking Thing
To This Fucked Up World
Famous Puppet – Famous Puppet
Peace Of Mind – In A Peaceful World
Is What We Want – So Fuck Off
Let Them Have Their Minds Back

Dirty-Hands – Dirty-Minds
We-Are-Human – We-Are-Flawed
God-Did-Not – Bless-Our-Souls
There is No-Devil in Hell's-Fire
Sin-Was-Created by Man
Live-For-The – Fucking-Day
Like-There is No-Fucking – Tomorrow
Unless-You-Have – Something-Better to Do

(Chorus)
Famous Puppet – Famous Puppet
Look At You Over There
With Your Skin Hanging Off You
Like You Mean a Fucking Thing
To This Fucked Up World
Famous Puppet – Famous Puppet
Peace Of Mind – In A Peaceful World
Is What We Want – So Fuck Off F. Puppets
Let Them Have Their Minds Back
43

Love Beams (843.A) (Gemini's Version)
(Written 09/17/2015)

Baby-Do-You – Want to Take a Trip
Catch-Yourself – Some-Love-Beams
That-Will-Ripple – Through-Your-Body
Like a Love-Stream of Hot-Ecstasy

I've-Got – You're-Destination
Give-You a Chance to Purr
On-This-Full-Moon – Love-Beam-Night

(Chorus)
Love-Beams – Love-Beams
Makes Everything All Right
Love-Beams – Love-Beams
Makes You Lose Control
Love-Beams – Love-Beams
Will Make You Forget Everything But Passion
Love-Beams – Love-Beams
Will Make You Addicted To My Love

Baby-Do-You – Want to Take a Trip
Catch-Yourself – Some-Love-Beams
That-Will-Ripple – Through-Your-Body
Like a Love-Stream of Hot-Ecstasy

I've-Got – You're-Destination
Give-You a Chance to Purr
On-This-Full-Moon – Love-Beam-Night

(Chorus)
Love-Beams – Love-Beams
Makes Everything All Right
Love-Beams – Love-Beams
Makes You Lose Control
Love-Beams – Love-Beams
Will Make You Forget Everything But Passion
Love-Beams – Love-Beams
Will Make You Addicted To My Love

Love Beams (843.B) (Starblue's Version)
(Written 09/18/2015)

I come to you from a dimension,
That's filled with love.
I bring with me,
No sadness nor pain.
I only bring you love.

(Chorus)
Feel it, feel my love beams.
Let them fill you full of love.
Feel it, feel my love beams.
Let them mend your broken heart.
Feel it, feel my love beams.
Let them re-introduce you to love.

I love your smile,
I love your laugh.
We are happy,
We are in love.
Together we shine
Bright as a blue star.

(Chorus)
Feel it, feel my love beams.
Let them fill you full of love.
Feel it, feel my love beams.
Let them mend your broken heart.
Feel it, feel my love beams.
Let them re-introduce you to love.

Oh' Weed (946.)
(Written 8/10/2016)

When-I – Wanna-Feel-Better
You're-Always – There-For-Me
Just-Being – What-You-Are
Making-Me-High – With-Your-Sweet-Buds

The-Scent – You-Give-Off
Brings-Back – My-Yesterdays
The-Good – The-Bad
But-That's-Okay
'Cause-You – Were-There
To-Make-Me – Feel-Better
Whenever – I-Wanted-It

(Chorus)
Oh Weed – Oh Weed
You Beautiful Green Weed
You're From Mother Earth
Oh Weed – Oh Weed
I Don't Know Why
So Many Hate You So Much
When All You Wanna Do Is Help
Oh Weed – Get Me High

When-I – Wanna-Feel-Better
You're-Always – There-For-Me
Just-Being – What-You-Are
Making-Me-High – With-Your-Sweet-Buds

(Chorus)
Oh Weed – Oh Weed
You Beautiful Green Weed
You're From Mother Earth
Oh Weed – Oh Weed
I Don't Know Why
So Many Hate You So Much
When All You Wanna Do Is Help
Oh Weed – Get Me High

Don't Grope Me (998.)
(Written 12/04/2017)

Hello – Mister-Producer
Hello – Mister- Actor
Hello – Mister-Politician
Hello – Mister-Wall-Street

Let-Me-Tell-You – What
What is What – You-Want to Know
Listen-Very-Carefully – You'll-Find-Out
Now-First – All of You
Put-You-Hands in Your-Pockets
So-I-Can – Begin

(Chorus)
Don't Grope Me
You Horny Men And Bastards
If I Want You To – I'll Let You Know
But Don't Count On It
So Don't Grope Me
I'm Here To Do My Job
Not Be Your Next Sex Moment
Do You Understand What I'm Saying
If You Don't You Better
Leave Your Hands In Your Pockets
Because I Don't Want To Be Groped By You

Hello – Mister-Producer
Hello – Mister- Actor
Hello – Mister-Politician
Hello – Mister-Wall-Street

Yes-I'm a Sexy-Lady
Yes – This is Very-True
But-That – Doesn't-Give-You
The-Right to Grope-Me
Just-Because – You-Want to
So-Listen to Me – One-More-Time

(Repeat Chorus)

Short Story #1: Tirg and Seralena
(Pages 48-53)

"I don't want to go mother."

"You will go Seralena and you will be the perfect Princess that your kingdom expects you to be."

"Mother, please Tirg is so ugly. I can't sit there beside him all night like I want to be there."

"Seralena, do not let that pretty face of yours go to your head. It does not matter to the kingdom nor should it matter to you how Prince Tirg looks. All that matters is that he is a Prince, a very wealthy and powerful Prince, from a kingdom that our kingdom would be held in high regard after your marriage to him."

"Marriage? Never. I'm starting to feel sick inside just thinking of it. Mother how could I ever let someone that looks like Tirg lay his ugly body on top of mine?"

"Very easy Seralena, because of your beauty it will be a blessing to you. Take it from me Seralena, just lie there and try to ignore the sounds you hear, for like I say, your looks will make what you have to endure go faster for you. Prince Tirg will love you very much. If you can become a smart woman, by using your means to their very highest then your beauty will allow you to be a woman that has a lot of power, perhaps enough power to wrap your Prince and future King around your fingers."

"Mother I do not care about power. Mother all I care about is love. I want to be in love with a handsome man, I don't care if he's a Prince, I don't even care if he is poor."

"You stupid girl! The world does not work like that. That love you want to feel will only come to you in your dreams. Now no more of this. I want you to pick out the dress that you will be wearing next Saturday night..."

"On the night that yours and Prince Tirg's engagement will be announced. Now do as your mother commands and try practicing your smile. I want you to look like your smile is painted on your pretty face."

Queen Mother leaves her daughter Princess Seralena, to vent out her frustrations over getting married to a pig of a man. She feels sad for her daughter but part of her is jealous of her daughter's great looks. So after a bit of sadness comes a smile across her lips, knowing that her daughter will be knocked down from out of the sky of life that she has been living so far and all because her father the King adores his daughter above anything else.

The King is mad about his beautiful daughter marrying a pig of a Prince like Prince Tirg. Mother Queen smiles even wider, knowing that it was her efforts that changed her King's mind. All it took was for her to point out the weaknesses of their kingdom and what their daughter's marriage could provide to strengthen them.

Princess Seralena is alone in her room crying her eyes out. 'I have to get myself out of this Hell. There is no way I will be married to anyone that I do not Love. Why me? Why me? He is so ugly, he will want a kiss. Stop it, get that pig out of your mind Seralena, you have to do some fast thinking.'

The next day, Princess Seralena is deep in the middle of poor town with all its bandits and outlaws present for her to check out. She talks to many before eyeing one outlaw whose looks are as great as his sternness and scarred body.

"Do you know who I am?"

"Yes, you are Princess Seralena the most beautiful of all Princess."

"Very good, now clear us a table so I can tell you what I

want you to do for me."

"Very well Princess, however I do not work for free." Mirc walks over to a table with four drinkers occupying it, kicks one of the drinkers in the face knocking him to the floor, then does the same to a second drinker. The third and fourth drinkers look at the other, they both grab their drink stand up and run away very fast. "What can I do for you Princess?"

"I want you to remove Prince Tirg from my life."

"Remove?"

"Yes remove."

"That is a very polite way of putting it Princess. You can say remove if you want but don't fool yourself. What you want me to do Princess is very dark and final."

"I am quite aware of that Mr. Mirc."

"Are you Princess? There is no going back or changing your mind. I will do this for you but I have to be Dead sure that you do not have second thoughts and I end up with my head on a block while looking up at the axe man as he is readying himself to chop it off."

"I have a lot of money Mirc. So whatever your price is, I can give it to you."

"Yes money and gold. Lots of it will be my price. But there is one more thing that I demand from you if you want my favor."

"And what is that Mirc?"

"Your body!"

"What? How dare you? I should have your head for even

thinking about my precious body like that."

"Then Princess go find you another to do your bidding, for it shall not be I."

"Wait a minute. There has to be another way?"

"No. No other way. This is what I demand. Your body. I will enjoy it first just in case I fail, which has never happened or in case you are a bad Princess, looking to live dangerously."

"I assure you Mirc I am not doing this on some whim. I will not marry Prince Tirg. I'd rather see him dead or start a war or even die before I let him touch me. Mirc he is so ugly, you have to help me escape this life."

"Well then Seralena give me your body and I will set you free to journey on to find love for yourself."

"I can't, I just can't. You have the devil in your soul Mirc. I guess for my future, better once with a devil than a lifetime with a pig."

Seralena for the very first time makes love. Mirc tries his best to treat Seralena like the Princess she is. Her touch, her flame makes him want to own her, she is like no one before. So gentle, so trusting.

Mirc will be glad to remove anyone from Seralena's life that she does not like and out of his path, so Seralena will become his wife. Mirc gets up and walks away thinking to himself after they are done making love for the third time in as many hours.

'Her father would see me dead, if I were to just look too long at her. King's got to go. Here let me practice. Seralena, I am so sorry about your father the King. He was a great King but now he's dead and gone and my sweet Seralena I am here to take you away from sadness

51

by becoming your King my future loving Queen. Sounds great. I can't believe it, with all the killings I have done in war and as an outlaw, I always thought that the high point of my life would be because I was a warrior. Love. I have loved so many I cannot even remember them all...'

'Seralena, I love her, I know she loves me now. I am her first and Heaven help me I will be her only. I will turn around and look at her, giving her the chance to look at the greatness, that turned her into a woman, that is under my complete control.'

Mirc turns around to see and hears this. Seralena is getting dressed and looks at Mirc, "Is that it then? You are done? No need to answer, you are done. This better more than assure you of my resolve. Now go do your thing Outlaw. I have to tell you this Outlaw before you leave, you were good enough well at some points you were almost enjoyable. But to experience the same thing with Trig, I'd rather run away with you. What a joke that would be, would it not Outlaw?"

"Seralena."

"That is Princess Seralena to you Outlaw. What dare you have in you to say just my name to me after defiling me like this, Outlaw."

(Silence.) "Well say your words Outlaw."

"Princess Seralena, I love you. I want to be your King, and for you to be my Queen."

"Love me? I know all too well Mirc but to be my King and I your Queen, that would only happen in your dreams. Now go do your worst, then come back to me for your payment, your payment that will be quite less than you asked for. Better yet Outlaw, you will get no money at all instead, I will let you make love to me one more time. After that I better never lay eyes on you again until I send for you, just in case my future king lacks passion."

"Yes Princess Seralena, my heart, body and soul belong to you forever."

"I know and I don't want either of them. I just want your passionate obedience. How was I Outlaw?"

"Fine enough for me to put up with all your shit."

Book Nineteen: Fucked Up (Pages 54-82)

(Side One)
361. Fucked Up (785.)
-----. Kiss My Happy Ass (814.) (Bonus)
362. It's Time To Rest Now (721.)
363. I Don't Give A Damn (723.)
364. I Live My Life For Myself (728.)
365. Can You Feel It (729.)

(Side Two)
366. Freedom Cost More Than Money (732.)
367. The Devil Can Kiss My Ass (733.)
368. Maybe You're Not Insane /
-----. Run (Go Catch Yourself) (734.)
369. Death Junkie / Dead Bastard (736.)
370. Death Devil (739.)

(Side Three)
371. I Drink Because I Can (741.)
372. Eat Crap And Like It (742.)
373. You Sad Sack Of Crap (747.)
374. Warriors Blood (751.)
375. Crapped Out Freedoms (752.)

(Side Four)
376. To Your Grave You Go # Next (753.)
377. Cold Inside (760.)
378. Crammed (786.)
379. Smashed (787.)
380. Thrashed (788.)

(Bonus Songs)
Death Is On My Heels #1 (789.)
Death Is On My Heels #2 (790.)
Purgatory (20 Steps) (The Single) (100.)

Lyrical Stories Melody: **(Pages 83-98)**
Short Story #2: Space-Sex = Space Clap **(Pages 99-103)**

361. Fucked Up

They-Burn-The-Sky – They-Poison-The-Water
Peace is For-Fools / When-Death-Rules-The-World

Love's a Four-Letter-Word / Sex is Up – In-The-Market
Take a Picture of Yourself – Trade-Your-Head – With-Your-Ass
Play-The-Game – Another-Day and Night – Fuck-That

(Chorus)
I Don't Know – But I Think
The World Is Fucked Up
Maybe I'm Wrong – But
I Believe This Very Strongly
What Do You Think
Is The World Fucked Up – Or
Is It Bleeding To Death – Just Fine

God-Says-No – Devil-Says-Yes – Feed-The-Poor
Tax-Them-More – So-Many-Choices – Hard to Decide
Head-Hurts-Bad – Fuck-This

Where's-My-Bed – I-Can't-Sleep
Turn on The-News – Same-Fucked-Up-Stuff
I-Should-Feed-My-Face – It's-Not-Hungry
Lights go Out – As-I – Stare at The-Darkness
Damn-I'm so Turned-Off – Fuck-This

(Chorus)
I Don't Know – But I Think
The World Is Fucked Up
Maybe I'm Wrong – But
I Believe This Very Strongly
What Do You Think
Is The World Fucked Up – Or
Is It Bleeding To Death – Just Fine

Come-On-Everybody – Sing-This
Fucked-Up – The-World-Is-Fucked-Up
What-Can-We – Fucking-Do-About-It
Fucked-Up – The-World-Is-Fucked-Up
Maybe-Nothing – But-More and More-Fucking
Fucked-Up – The-World-Is-Fucked-Up
What's-Wrong – Are-You – Turned Off-Like-Me
55

Kiss My Happy Ass (814.) (Bonus)

I-Was-Down – Down-I-Was
I-Was-Limp – Limp-I-Was
Life-Was-Kicking – My-Ass
Making-Me its Dirty-Bastard

Didn't-Know – What to Do
I-Tried – Drinking
I-Tried – Smoking
Then – I-Got-Laid
Has-My-Life – Changed
I-Damn-Well – Want-It to Stay-This-Way
So-Here's to Getting-Laid

(Chorus)
Happy – I'm Happy Today
I Washed All My Funk
Right Down The Freaking Drain
Happy – I'm Happy Today
Hate – Sadness And Fear
Can Kiss My Happy Ass
Because – I'm Getting Laid Again

Blood and War – Stay-Away
Doom and Damnation – Stay-Away
Better-Yet – Kiss-My-Ass
'Cause-You're-Nothing – Besides-Trash

If-You-Don't – Like-Me-Getting-Laid
Then-Turn – Your-Stupid-Heads
'Cause-I-Will-Shake – My-Getting-Laid-Ass
Right-In-Your – Stupid-Faces

(Chorus)
Happy – I'm Happy Today
I Washed All My Funk
Right Down The Freaking Drain
Happy – I'm Happy Today
Hate – Sadness And Fear
Can Kiss My Happy Ass
Because – I'm Getting Laid Again

362. It's Time To Rest Now

Good – Bad – Is-There a Difference
When an Infection – Has-Entered
The-Minds of Humanity – Flawed-Made
Thoughts of Millions – Extorted by Believing
In-The-Lies of Them

One by One – We-March to No-Hope
Knowing – Our-Day-Will-Come
While-Freedom – Waves its Hands
That-Are-Dirty – Stained-Thick
With-The-Blood of The-Innocent

(Chorus)
It's My Time To Rest Now
Freedom Is Not Needed Anymore
It's My Time To Rest Now
Nothingness Is Creeping Up On Me
It's My Time To Rest Now
My Time – To Feed The Clay

Old and Older – We've-Become
As-They-Stayed – Fresh and Clean
While-Guilty as Charged is Stamped
On-Our-Backs – With-Force
Like-It's-Still – Common-Place

Speak-Up – Put-On a List
Stay-Still – Stay-Unknown
Freedom-Cost-You – Your-Freedom
Every-Known – Controlled-Day
'Til-The-Day – You-Are – No-Longer-Here

(Chorus)
It's My Time To Rest Now
Freedom Is Not Needed Anymore
It's My Time To Rest Now
Nothingness Is Creeping Up On Me
It's My Time To Rest Now
My Time – To Feed The Clay

363. I Don't Give A Damn

I-Was-Born-Poor as Can-Be
Having – Food – Sometimes
Having – No-Bed to Sleep-In
Hardly-Ever

I-Prayed at Night – I-Cried at Night
I-Grew-Up-Strong on The-Outside
Knowing-That – I'm-The-Only-One
That-Cares – If-I-Live or If-I-Die

(Chorus)
I Am Dirty – I Am Horny
I Don't Give A Damn
Eat My Crap – People
That Want Me To Clean Up
So I Can Be Just Like You

Beating-Hard-Heart – Fire in My-Soul
I-Live – My-Way – Forever
I-Don't-Need-You – You-Need-Me

I-Am-Freedom – That-Won't-Change
You-Are-Ready
To-Become – Something-New
When-The-World – Changes-Its-Mood

(Chorus)
I Am Dirty – I Am Horny
I Don't Give A Damn
Eat My Crap – People
That Want Me To Clean Up
So I Can Be Just Like You

What-Can-I-Say – You-Are-Weak
In-The-Waiting to Pull-Off-Another
Layer of Yourself – For-The-Man to Own
While-I-Stay – Whole and Strong
In-The-Waiting – For-More-Freedom to Own

(Repeat Chorus)

58

364. I Live My Life For Myself

Come-On – Let's-Go
Let's-Lose – Control
Our-Bodies – Are-Stiff
Our-Beings – Are-Fading
Faith-Is a Joke – From-Day-One

Come-On – Let's-Go
Let's-Lose – Control
Freedom – Can-Only be Obtained
When-There's-No – Heaven or Hell

(Chorus)
I Live My Life For Myself
I Don't Need A God
To Damn Me For Being Myself
I Live My Life For Myself
I Don't Need A God
Getting In My Way – While Getting Laid

Come-On – Let's-Go
Let's-Lose – Control
Hell-With-Them – For-Damning-Us
They-Won't-Change – Forever
They-Like-Themselves – This-Way

Come-On – Let's-Go
Let's-Lose – Control
We-Only-Have – One-Life to Live
Would-You-Rather – Pray to God
Or-Have-Sinning – Sex-With-We
That-Will-Change-You – Forevermore

(Chorus)
I Live My Life For Myself
I Don't Need A God
To Damn Me For Being Myself
I Live My Life For Myself
I Don't Need A God
Getting In My Way – While Getting Laid

365. Can You Feel It

Do-You-Have-It – Do-I
I-Can't-Remember – Anymore
Seems-To-Be a Word – With-No-Meaning
That-Has-Been – Taken-Away – From-Us

I-Have-Been-Cut – I-Have-Bled
Crimes – Have-Been-Committed
Not-By-Me – It's-Always-Them
Yet-They-Are-Never – Guilty as Charged

(Chorus)
Can You Feel It
The Lost They Have Brought Us
Can You Feel It
Freedom Is A Dead Thought Now
Can You Feel It
We're So Damned Screwed

Forever-Is a Long-Time
Lady-Liberty is Crying
Why is She – Hated so Much
When-Nothing-Else – Makes-Sense

I-Am-One – You-Are-One
Together – We-Are-Two
Hey-Everyone – Come-Over-Here
Let's-Do-Some-Freedom – Resurrecting
Let's-Make – The-Corrupted-Pay
For-Their-Crimes – Against-Our-Freedoms

(Chorus)
Can You Feel It
The Lost They Have Brought Us
Can You Feel It
Freedom Is A Dead Thought Now
Can You Feel It
We're So Damned Screwed

366. Freedom Cost More Than Money

Blood on Your-Shoes
Blood on Your-Soul
Take-Their-Crap
Remember to Smile – Everyday
Until-The-Day – You-Die

Pay-Their-Taxes – On-Time
Give-Them a Thank-You
You'll be Put – On a Friends-List
That-You-Can – Show-Off to Everyone

(Chorus)
One More Day
And You'll Be Free
You're A Dumb Ass
If You Believe This – Because
Freedom Cost More Than Money
Freedom Cost More Than You Have

Alone-In a Crowd
Your-Mind is Screaming
As-Your-Ass is Itching
Can't-Get-Away – From-Them
They-Know – Your-Name

Your-Sanctuary is Tainted-With
Pictures of Them – On-Your-Walls
How-Do-You – Get-Out of This
Before it Makes – You-Die
I-Don't-Know – I'm-Dead
Talking to You – From-My-Grave

(Chorus)
One More Day
And You'll Be Free
You're A Dumb Ass
If You Believe This – Because
Freedom Cost More Than Money
Freedom Cost More Than You Have

367. The Devil Can Kiss My Ass

I'm-Dying – Kiss-My-Ass – World
My-Blood – Has-Turned to Ice
Everything is Melting-Away
Eyesight – Out of Focus
Is-That-Death – Coming-My-Way

Hey-Death – Kiss-My-Ass
Keep-Your-Hands – Off-My-Soul
I'm-Pissed – I-Want to Live
Not-Die and Go to Hell

(Chorus)
The Devil Can Kiss My Ass
The Soulless Bastard
Who Is He To Own My Soul
My Soul Belongs To Me – So
The Devil Can Kiss My Ass
I'll Kick Open The Gates
And Walk My Soul Right Out Of Hell

1 – 2 – 3 – Die-Very-Soon
All by My – Freaking-Self
Dump-It – Dump-Everything
I'm-Not-Going to Take-This-Crap
I-Guess-God – Hates-Me

Can't-Go to Heaven – Don't-Belong-In-Hell
What-Can-One-Man's – Soul-Do
I-Got-It – Take-Away – Some-From-Both
What-The-Freak-Out – Should-I
Call-My-New – Home

(Chorus)
The Devil Can Kiss My Ass
The Soulless Bastard
Who Is He To Own My Soul
My Soul Belongs To Me – So
The Devil Can Kiss My Ass
I'll Kick Open The Gates
And Walk My Soul Right Out Of Hell

368. Maybe You're Not Insane / Run (Go Catch Yourself)

The-Spider – Eats-The-Fly
As a Rainbow – Starts to Bleed
Your-Mind is Dying – From-Insanity
Lick-The-Moon – Eat-Some-Grass
Maybe – You're – Not – Insane

Laughing-At a Hole in The-Floor
Your-Tongue – Gets-Very-Thick
As-Your-Nose – Squirts-Out-Blood
That-You Dance-On – So-Wildly

(Chorus #1)
Maybe You're Not Insane
Maybe This Is A Dream
Maybe You Can Wake Up
Maybe You Should Kiss Your
Mind Goodbye – To Insanity's Grasp

Orange – Stained – Taffy
Dunked-In – Your-Eyes
As-Your-Fingerprints – Slide-Off
Leaving-You a Nobody
Run – Go-Catch-Yourself

Jackal-People – Did-You a Favor
Playing-With-Your – Helpless-Mind
The-River-Styx – Flows-Clear and Red
As-You-Begin to Smile – Big and Wide

(Chorus #2)
Run – Go Catch Yourself
Maybe – He's Got Your Sanity
Run – Go Catch Yourself
Maybe – He Will Like You
Run – Go Catch Yourself
Maybe – He Will Hate You
Run – Go Catch Yourself
Too Late Your Mind Is Dead

369. Death Junkie / Dead Bastard

Life-Is a Pain – In-The-Life
As-You – Crave-Your-Grave
No-Time to Laugh – No-Time for Sex
Unless-It's-Filled – With-Pain

Black – Leather – Teddies
Barbwire – Wrapped-Around – Her-Body
You-Lick-Up – Every-Drop of Blood
That-She – Spills-Out – On-The-Floor

(Chorus #1)
Death Junkie – Death Junkie
Will Take You – To Your Grave
Death Junkie – Death Junkie
Wipes Your Blood – On Their Life
Death Junkie – Death Junkie
Eats – Sleeps – And Loves Death
Death Junkie – Death Junkie
Why Can't You – Just Kill Yourself

Door-Comes – Crashing-Open
Blue-People – Running-In
Bullets-Land in Your-Body
As-You – Drop to Your-Death

Picked-Up – Like-Garbage
Thrown-In-The-Ground
No-Prayers – Only a Stray-Dog
Pissing-On-Your – Lonely-Grave

(Chorus #2)
Dead Bastard – Dead Bastard
Dead In The Ground
Dead Bastard – Dead Bastard
You Killed So Many Women
Dead Bastard – Dead Bastard
I Hope You Rot In Pain
Dead Bastard – Dead Bastard
You Will Become – The Devil's Bitch

370. Death Devil

One-Day – You-Are-Happy and Free
Then – Out of Nowhere
Death-Devil – Rips at Your-Soul

You-Bleed – From-Your-Mouth
You-Bleed – From-Your-Ass
Not-Knowing – What is Happening to You

Test – Test – Are-You-Dying – Today
Will-You – Wait-'Til – Tomorrow
Why-Has-God – Forsaken-You

(Chorus)
Death Devil – Death Devil
Scratching At Your Soul
Death Devil – Death Devil
Lives In Burning Hell
Death Devil – Death Devil
Eats Your Soul Then Laughs
Death Devil – Death Devil
Doesn't Give A Hell About You

One-Day – You-Are-Happy and Free
Then – Out of Nowhere
Death Devil – Rips at Your-Soul

Boredom and Snacking – Is-Why
Death-Devil is Eating-Your-Soul
Your-Soul is Fading-Away to Nothing
Your-Mind – Understands-Why
All-Because – You're a Sinner – Going to Hell

(Chorus)
Death Devil – Death Devil
Scratching At Your Soul
Death Devil – Death Devil
Lives In Burning Hell
Death Devil – Death Devil
Eats Your Soul Then Laughs
Death Devil – Death Devil
Doesn't Give A Hell About You

371. I Drink Because I Can

Wake-Up – Shaking in Pain
Alone – Can't-Find – My-Clothes
Head-Feels – Soft and Thick
I-Did-It-Again! – Drinking
Myself-Into-Numbing – Happiness

Need a Drink – I-Need-Three
Damn-The-Pain of My-Life
Will-I – Ever-Learn
Do-I – Give a Damn
(Pause) No – I – Don't

(Chorus)
I Drink Because I Can
If You Can't Hang With Me
Get The Hell Out Of My Way
I Drink Because I Can
I Don't Need You
All I Need Is – Alcohol
A Fine Lady To Drive Me Home
Have Sex With Me – Then Leave

I'm-The-Heartless – Bastard
That-Hates-Life – Unless-I'm-Drunk
Then-It's-This-World – That-Is a Heartless-Bastard
I'm-The-Normal – Above-Board and Ready-For-Sex

Open-Bar – Hell-Yeah
Bet-I-Drink and Score
Hey-Baby – Love-Me – For-My-Body
Not-For-My-Drunk – Don't-Kiss-Me – Lips

(Chorus)
I Drink Because I Can
If You Can't Hang With Me
Get The Hell Out Of My Way
I Drink Because I Can
I Don't Need You
All I Need Is – Alcohol
A Fine Lady To Drive Me Home
Have Sex With Me – Then Leave

372. Eat Crap And Like It

Kill-Somebody – Just-Like-That
Eat-Crap – And-Like-It
Rape-For – Sex-Hate
Eat-Crap – And-Like-It
Slice-People-In-Two
Eat-Crap – And-Like-It
Hate-Because of Color
Eat-Crap – And-Like-It
Hate-The-Homeless – Hate-The-Junkies
Eat-Crap – And-Like-It
Hate-Those – That-Don't-Believe
Eat-Crap – And-Like-It

(Chorus)
You Are So Crapped Up – We Hate You
So Very Much – Eat Crap And Like It
You Are So Crapped Up – We Hate You
So Very Much – Eat Crap And Like It
Do You Understand – You Sacks Of Crap

Kill-Somebody – Just-Like-That
Eat-Crap – And-Like-It
Rape-For – Sex-Hate
Eat-Crap – And-Like-It
Slice-People-In-Two
Eat-Crap – And-Like-It
Hate-Because of Color
Eat-Crap – And-Like-It
Hate-The-Homeless – Hate-The-Junkies
Eat-Crap – And-Like-It
Hate-Those – That-Don't-Believe
Eat-Crap – And-Like-It
Hate-Those – That-Like to Do-Themselves
Eat-Crap – And-Like-It

(Chorus)
You Are So Crapped Up – We Hate You
So Very Much – Eat Crap And Like It
You Are So Crapped Up – We Hate You
So Very Much – Eat Crap And Like It
Do You Understand – You Sacks Of Crap

373. You Sad Sack Of Crap

Slap-Your-Ass to Wake-Up – Your-Brain
Life is Laughing – In-Your-Face
All-You-Do -is- For-Nothing
Did-You – Make a Mistake – On-The-Day
You-Let-Your-Mind – Slip-Away

Fantasy is Sexy-Dangerous
Reality-Bites – The-Big-One
Who-Cares – Crap-Filled-Minded

(Chorus)
Tomorrow Is Another Day
Wipe The Dust Off Your Ass
You Sad Sack Of Crap
Tomorrow Is Another Day
Wipe The Dust Off Your Ass
You Sad Sack Of Crap
Tomorrow Is Another Day
For You To Beep Up Once Again

Big-O' 747 – In-The-Sky
No – You-Can-Not – Bite-It
Let-Me – Hear-Your – Battle-Cry
From-Your-Half-Dead – Lonely-Mind
Rust-Never-Sleeps – Do-You

Fantasy is Sexy-Dangerous
Reality-Bites – The-Big-One
Who-Cares – Crap-Filled-Minded

(Chorus)
Tomorrow Is Another Day
Wipe The Dust Off Your Ass
You Sad Sack Of Crap
Tomorrow Is Another Day
Wipe The Dust Off Your Ass
You Sad Sack Of Crap
Tomorrow Is Another Day
For You To Beep Up Once Again

374. Warriors Blood

I-Was-Trained to Kill
I-Was-Needed to Win-The-War
I-Am a Warrior – In a Uniform

My-Rifle – Will-Save – My-Life
My-Rifle – Will-Kill – Many-Enemies
Uncle-Sam – Sure-Does-Love-Me

(Chorus)
Warrior's Blood
Bleeding On The Ground
Warrior's Blood
Have You Forgotten Me
Warrior's Blood
I'm Coming Home – Battle Scarred

Shoot-First – Shoot-Last
They-Fear – No-Warriors
We-Are-The-Evil – That-Needs to Die

Freedom – They-Hate – Today
Freedom – They-Hate – Tomorrow
Never-Surrender – Just-More-War
Just-More-Hate – For the U.S.A.

(Chorus)
Warrior's Blood
Bleeding On The Ground
Warrior's Blood
Have You Forgotten Me
Warrior's Blood
I'm Coming Home – Battle Scarred

I-Fought – I-Lost – My-Arm
I-Fought – I-Lost – My-Leg
Where is Our – Welcome-Back – Heroes
America-Sure-Does – Love-Us so Very-Much

(Repeat Chorus)

69

375. Crapped Out Freedoms

Can't-You – See the Evil in Their-Eyes
Can't-You – Feel the Evil in Their-Hearts
They-Are – The-Privileged in Control
That-Eat-Up-Freedoms – Without-Chewing

Why-Do-You – Bring-Them – Salt
Why-Do-You – Bring-Them – Pepper
When – You-Should be Giving-Them
Your-Foot – Up-Their-Asses
At-Least – Your-Middle-Finger
Right-In-Their-Privileged – Faces

(Chorus)
Where The Hell Is Our Freedoms
They Ate Them All Up – That's Where
I Guess We Can Follow Them Around
Maybe They Will Crap Them Back Out
Then Again Do We Really Want
Crapped Out Freedoms – To Use And Own

They-Start-Wars – That-They – Don't-Finish
Time's-Up – Let's-All-Go-Home
Ten-Years-Later – We're-Back-There-Again

What's-Wrong – With-American-Pride
What's-Wrong – With-Apple-Pie
Our-Enemies – Are-Suppose to Hate-Us
Not – Our – Government

It's-Not-Our-Fault – They-Keep-On – Screwing-Up
Vote – Vote – Vote – All-These-A-Holes – Out
Or-They – Will-Eat – America-All-Up – Then-Burp
Saying-It's-Our-Fault – That-They – Have-Gas

(Chorus)
Where The Hell Is Our Freedoms
They Ate Them All Up – That's Where
I Guess We Can Follow Them Around
Maybe They Will Crap Them Back Out
Then Again Do We Really Want
Crapped Out Freedoms – To Use And Own

376. To Your Grave You Go # Next

Traveling in Space – Alone and Free
Having-My – Death-Stubs – Get-Punched
Eating the Remains of Some-Carcass
From-The-Last – Planet-I-Scored
Real-Big and Thick

I-Like-It – Like-That
Fun-In-The-Sun – Sex – And a Contract
Another-One-Down – The-Thicker-My-Wallet
The-Finer-The-Ladies – Who-Wants to Party

(Chorus)
I Come – I Kill – I Get Paid
To Your Grave You Go # Next
Low Life – Cream Of The Crop
I Don't Give A Laser Blast
'Cause All I Want Is Money And Ladies
To Your Grave You Go # Next
I Don't Even Give A Damn – If You Burn In Hell

You-Must-Have – Pissed-Someone-Off
For-I, to Come-For-You – I'm-Expensive
Never a Sorry – It's-The-Game – I-Play
With-The-Winning-Hand – Every-Time

Scream – Beg – Offer-Me – Your-Woman
Even-More-Money – Does-No-Good
I-Have a One-Track-Mind – Work – Paid – Playthings
Then-It's-Back to Traveling in Space
Having-My – Death-Stubs – Get-Punched

(Chorus)
I Come – I Kill – I Get Paid
To Your Grave You Go # Next
Low Life – Cream Of The Crop
I Don't Give A Laser Blast
'Cause All I Want Is Money And Ladies
To Your Grave You Go # Next
I Don't Even Give A Damn – If You Burn In Hell

377. Cold Inside

Warmth – Filled-My-Heart
Enlightenment – Filled-My-Soul
But-Now – I-Feel so Cold-Inside
Like – I've-Already-Died

Sun-Shines – Down on Me
Might as Well be The-Moon
For-Its-Beams – Bounce-Off
Like-It's Just a Facade – Just to Let
Me-Know – Something's-Not-Right

(Chorus)
I Feel So Cold Inside
Where Is My Spark Of Life
How Did It Get Burned Out
I Was Doing So Great
Then One Day – Doom And Gloom
Like I Am A – Dead Man Walking

I-Don't-Know – How to Feel-Alive
Tried-This – Tried-That – No-Good
Strangers – Keep-On – Just-Walking-By
Like-They – Do-Not-See or Hear-Me
Wait a Minute – I-Don't – Have a Heartbeat

(Chorus)
I Feel So Cold Inside
Where Is My Spark Of Life
How Did It Get Burned Out
I Was Doing So Great
Then One Day – Doom And Gloom
Like I Am A – Dead Man Walking

There's-This-Bright – Light in The-Sky
Shining-Down – Just-For-Me to Feel
Too-Bad – I-Don't-Care – Anymore
Think-I'll – Just-Keep-On – Walking-Along
Maybe-Next-Time – I'll-Jump – Into-The-Sky

(Repeat Chorus)

72

378. Crammed

You-Want-Yes – They-Give-You-No
You go Home – The-Love of Your-Life
Still-Your-Yes – Is a Sad-No

Up is Down – Left is Right
Are-You – Suppose to Like to Sin
Since-Everything is Backwards

Oil-Mixed in Your-Water
Matches-The-Calm and Insane
That-Blinks – In-Only-One-Eye

(Chorus)
No Is Crammed In Your Mind
No Is Crammed On Your Back
Making Your Life Really Suck
You're A Happy Yes Person
Stuck In A Sad World Of No

Yes is No – Can-No – Be-Yes
Do-Nothing and Save-The-World
Give a Helping-Hand
You-Damn-It-Forever

Enjoy-Yourself – Not-Wanting-It
Then-Get-Exactly – What-You-Want
Shake-Your-Head as Hard as You-Can

Confusion – May-Help-You-Cope
As-You-Turn – Into a No-Person
That-Wants to Save – The-World

(Chorus)
No Is Crammed In Your Mind
No Is Crammed On Your Back
Making Your Life Really Suck
You're A Happy Yes Person
Stuck In A Sad World Of No

379. Smashed

Go to Work – Work too Hard
Drag-My-Ass – Home
Feel-Like-Crap – Smell-Like-Crap
Stuff-My-Face – All-Full
Wash-My-Ass-Clean
I-Look so Ready to Party

Come on Baby – Ready and Willing
You-Can-Sit – Anywhere-You-Want
Then-We'll – Go-From-There

(Chorus)
She's Hot – I'm Drinking
She's Naked And Waiting
I'm Downing As Much As I Want
Don't Really Need It – I Just Like To
Get Smashed For A Few Hours
Then Give Her My Buzz To Enjoy

She-Says-Goodbye – I-Got-My-Beer
My-Buzz is Still – All-Good
What a Romp – She-Was
Can't-Think – Too-Smashed
I'm-Horny – Drunk and Ready

Where is My-Lady to Enjoy
That's-Right – She's-Long-Gone
I'll-Just Go-Outside – All-Naked
Damn-It's-Cold – Hey-Lady
I'm-Smashed – From-Here – You-Look
Like-You – Are-Good-Enough – For-The-Night

Excuse-Me-Officer – I'll-Go-Back-Inside
Go to Bed and Dream-About – Getting-Laid

(Chorus)
She's Hot – I'm Drinking
She's Naked And Waiting
I'm Downing As Much As I Want
Don't Really Need It – I Just Like To
Get Smashed For A Few Hours
Then Give Her My Buzz To Enjoy
74

380. Thrashed

Down-Deep – Into a Spiral of Confusion
Only-Had – Five-Drinks
Looks-Like – Trashed – Here-I-Come
Put-My-Hand on My-Everything
Got to Keep – My-Mind-Focused
Who-Knows – Who-Drugged-Me – Tonight

Floor is My-Bed – Oh-My-Head
Where-The-Hell – Am-I-This-Time
I'm-Naked – Looks-Like – I-Had a Good-Time
Clothes-Gone – Nowhere-In-Sight

(Chorus)
Just Wanted To Catch A Buzz
But Some Fucked Up Personality
Thrashed Me All Up – Left Me Naked
Making Me Find Anything Around
To Cover My Trashed And Used Body

Should-I-Go-Through – The-Humiliation
Tell-The-World – That-I – Don't-Know-Any-Better
Got to Make it Home and Safe
I'll-Be-Alright – After a Long-Washing
I'll-Pour-Myself a Drink
Because – I-Still-Feel-Dirty

(Chorus)
Just Wanted To Catch A Buzz
But Some Fucked Up Personality
Thrashed Me All Up – Left Me Naked
Making Me Find Anything Around
To Cover My Trashed And Used Body

I-Don't-Know – But-I-Think
The-World is Fucked-Up
Just-Wanted to Catch a Buzz
But-Some – Fucked-Up-Personality
Thrashed-Me-All-Up – Will-I-Ever-Learn
Not to Trust – In the Faith of Humanity

(Repeat Chorus)

(Bonus Song)

Death Is On My Heels #1 (789.)

Put-My-Guns – Away-Years-Ago
Wild-West is Where-I-Roamed
Whiskey – From-The-Bottle
Shooting – Blindly in The-Sky
Barmaids by The-Dozens
Everywhere-I-Go – Another-Body
For-Me to Put-Bullets-In

(Chorus)
Bullets In My Back
The Devil Is On My Tail
I Quit – They Brought Me Back In
Too Many Years – Un-Holstered
Now I Ride With The Wind
As Death Is On My Heels

I-Lived-Hard – I-Road-Hard
I-Was an Outlaw – I-Was a Lawman
I-Didn't-Give a Spit – Which-One
I-Had to Be – As-Long as I-Got-Paid
Hand-Me – My Reward – Open-Up-The-Safe
Cross-My-Path – Step-On-My-Boots
Steal-My-Horse – I'll-Fill-You – Full of Lead

(Chorus)
Bullets In My Back
The Devil Knows My Name
I Quit – They Brought Me Back In
Too Many Years – Un-Holstered
Now I Ride With The Wind
As Death Is On My Heels

Unhorsed – Left-For-Dead
Bleeding – From-Many-Holes
Don't-Think – Heaven-Wants-Me
Guess – I'll-Have to Settle-With
Riding-The-Fiery – Plains of Hell
Trying-For-Eternity – To-Out-Ride – The-Devil

(Repeat Chorus)
76

(Bonus Song)

Death Is On My Heels #2 (790.)

I-Fly in Fast – I-Fly in Hard
Always – Leave-Them-Guessing
If-It's-Their-Planet – I'll-Hit-Next
I'm-An-Outlaw of The-Galaxy
That-Leaves-Itself – Wide-Open – For-Me to Own
Woman-Troubles – Don't-Have-Them
'Cause-I-Always – Leave-Them-Crying
While-Their-Old-Man – Curses-My-Name

(Chorus)
Catch Me If You Can
My Space Ship Is Very Fast
I Guess It's My Own Fault
That Death Is On My Heels
But I Don't Give A Space-Crap
'Cause I'll Be A Space Outlaw
'Til The Day I Die – In Darkness Of Space
Holding On To Space-Gold – With Lipstick On My-Cheek

Space is Vast – Space is Cold
I-Only-Stop to Cause-Trouble
I-Steal – What-I-Want – From-Who-I-Want
I-Take-Their-Woman – For a Ride
In-My-Space-Ship – When-I'm-Done
I-Tell-Them – That-They're-Welcome
Then-Drop-Them-Off – Without-Looking-Back
'Cause – I've-Had-My-Fill and I-Don't-Want
Anymore of The-Same – Once-Again

(Chorus)
Catch Me If You Can
My Space Ship Is Very Fast
I Guess It's My Own Fault
That Death Is On My Heels
But I Don't Give A Space-Crap
'Cause I'll Be A Space Outlaw
'Til The Day I Die – In Darkness Of Space
Holding On To Space-Gold – With Lipstick On My-Cheek

Purgatory (20 Steps) (The Single) (100.)

Never-Really-Thought
Too-Much – About-The-Afterlife
Whether-There-Is a Heaven or Hell
Just-Lived-My-Life – For-The-Day
Did-Not – Hurt-Anyone
Didn't-Go-Out of My-Way
To-Do – Much-Good-Either

The-Way-I-Lived – My-Life
Brought-Me – One-Step-Closer
To-Purgatory – Didn't-Know-This
As-I-Found-Out – That-I
Had a Blood-Disorder
After-Becoming – Very-Sick
And-Thought – I-Was-Dying

Came to Find-Out – That-Was
My-First-Step – That-God-Made-For-Me
My-Second-Step – Came-When-I-Got
A-New-Pill – For-My-Condition
Worked-Great – Very-Fast
I-Was – Well-Again

My-Third-Step – Came-From-The-Combo
Of-My-Sickness and My-New-Pill
I-Saw-Angels – Made-No-Sense
Because-Nothing – Really-Came-From-It
Angels-Attacked-Me or Flew-Away
Later-On – They-Just-Ignored-Me – Entirely
If-This-Was a Seed – Nothing-Bloomed-From-It

(Chorus)
I Was Made By God
To Become Purgatory's Chosen One
By Killing Everyone And Sending Them To Hell
I Fell In Love Twice – I Was Betrayed And Killed
God Laughed As I Was Erased From Purgatory
And Sent To Hell To Take It Over For Him
After Ripping Off The Head Of Satan

78

My-Fourth-Step – God-Made-Me-Die
In a Burning – Car-Wreck – I-Do-Not
Remember-The-Pain – Just-The-Impact
My-Fifth-Step – Judgment – Sent to Purgatory
My-Sixth-Step – Goes-Along – With-My-Fifth-Step
I-Am-The-Last-One – That-Is-Allowed
To-Enter-Purgatory – It-Is-Now-Full

My-Seventh-Step – I-Feel-Since-I'm
The-Last-One – Allowed to Enter-Purgatory
That-Makes-Me-Special – Makes-Me-The-One
My-Eighth-Step – I and Everyone is Told
That-War-Is to Start – In-Purgatory
That-There-Can-Be – Only-One-Winner
I-Kill and I-Kill – Having so Much-Fun
Just so I-Can-Receive – My-Power-Ups
Which-Makes-Me – Stronger and Stronger

My-Ninth-Step – I-Am-Humbled
By a Cannibal – Hell-Witch
She-Ate-Some of Me – Tried to Kill-Me
But-Failed – I-Didn't-Kill-Her-Either
My-Tenth-Step – I-Became-Turned-On
Went to Find-What – Was-Turning-Me-On
The-Sweet-Scent – Lead-Me to The-Love-Den

Which-Led to My – Eleventh-Step
When-I-Fell – In-Love-Twice
A-Quick-Fantasy – My-Sweet-Angel-Eyes
Who-Betrayed-Me by Trying to Set-Me-Up
Then-Rebecka – The-One-That-Took
A-Long-Time to Become-Real and True
We-Lived – Our-Lives-Happily
Doing-Whatever – We-Wanted to Do

(Chorus)
I Was Made By God
To Become Purgatory's Chosen One
By Killing Everyone And Sending Them To Hell
I Fell In Love Twice – I Was Betrayed And Killed
God Laughed As I Was Erased From Purgatory
And Sent To Hell To Take It Over For Him
After Ripping Off The Head Of Satan

My-Twelfth-Step – The-Killing of My-Rebecka
The-Cannibal – Hell-Witch-Caught-Her
And-Ate-Her-All-Up – While-She-Was
Still-Alive – Rebecka-Drugged and Left-Me
The-Night-Before – I-Found-Her-Body
Rebecka-Was – No-Match for The-Witch

Hate-Brought-Forth – My-Thirteenth-Step
As-I-Killed – The-Cannibal-Hell-Witch
With-My-Spiked-Bat – I-Chopped-Her
Into-Pieces and Burned-Them to Ash

Tears-Brought – My-Fourteenth-Step
As-I-Spoke to My-Departed – Sweet-Rebecka
I-Made a Pledge to Her – With-My-Life
I-Would-Make-Everyone in Purgatory
Pay for Her-Death – With-Their-Lives

Which-Brought-Forth – My-Fifteenth-Step
A-Powerful-Rage-Up – That-Burns-Me-Out
As-Much as It – Powers-Me-Up
I-Was a Devastating – Killing-Machine
Killing-Hundreds – At a Time-With-Ease
Only-Way to Get – My-Super-Rage-Up
Out of Me – Was to Blow-Up a Mountain
That-Became – My-Sixteenth-Step
I-Now-Know – How to Tap – Into-My-Rage
Without it Taking – Too-Much-Out of Me

Free to Be – What-I-Have-Become
My-Seventeenth-Step – Brought-Me-Clarity
I-Was-Chosen by God to Win – The-War of Purgatory
And-Enter-His-Heaven – When-I-Was-Through
The-Biggest – Baddest-Ten of Us – Left
In-Purgatory – Have a Last-Battle to The-Death
I-Killed – Five of Them – Very-Bloodily
Making-Sure – I-Was the Last-One-Alive

80

(Chorus)
I Was Made By God
To Become Purgatory's Chosen One
By Killing Everyone And Sending Them To Hell
I Fell In Love Twice – I Was Betrayed And Killed
God Laughed As I Was Erased From Purgatory
And Sent To Hell To Take It Over For Him
After Ripping Off The Head Of Satan

So-Spent – I-Started to Reflect – My-Undeath
Which-Started to Bring in Sorrow
Wanting-Forgiveness – Given to Me
For-What-I – Was-made to Do – For-What
I-Had to Become to Win and Empty-Purgatory
Before-I-Could – Fully-Repent-My-Sins
The-Voice of God – Showed-Up and Pissed-Me-Off

Having-My-Own – Part-In-It – I-Helped
Bring-Fourth – My-Eighteenth-Step
With-Rage and Hatred-Inside-Me
I-No-Longer – Wanted-Forgiveness
I-Just-Wanted – My-Damn-Wings

Which-Was-What – God-Was-Waiting-For
Doing-This to Myself – Made-Me
Unworthy – No-Longer-Fit for Heaven
Now-No-One – From-Purgatory
Is-Allowed to Enter-Heaven

God-Brings-Forth a Killing-Present
Just for Me – My-Sweet-Angel-Eyes
Who-Was-Always an Angel
Sent to Purgatory by God to Entice-Me
My-Nineteenth-Step – Standing in Front of Me
My-Sweet-Angel-Eyes – Holding a Bone-White-Knife

I-Laugh-Out-Loud and Try to Kill-Her
But-None of My-Hits – Did-Any-Damage
Angel-Eyes – Stood-There-Silently
Staring at Me and Then-She-Stabbed-Me
In-My-Heart – With-Her-Angel's-Knife
Which-Kills-Me and Sends-Me to Hell

(Chorus)
I Was Made By God
To Become Purgatory's Chosen One
By Killing Everyone And Sending Them To Hell
I Fell In Love Twice – I Was Betrayed And Killed
God Laughed As I Was Erased From Purgatory
And Sent To Hell To Take It Over For Him
After Ripping Off The Head Of Satan

Before-I-Go to Hell – My-Twentieth-Step
My-Last-Step – From-God-Comes to Me
I-Am – Set-Loose on Hell – I'm to Enter
Kill as Many-Demons as I-Need – So-They
Step-Back – Obey-Me and Let-Me-Kill-Satan
God is Done-With-Me – I-Now-Rule-Hell for God
I-Tell-God – Where to Get-Off – I-Rule-My-Way

My – First – Step
God's-Unwanted – Twenty-First-Step
I-Attack – With-My-Army of Demons
Setting-Heaven on Fire

Dear-One and Only – Sweet-Forgiving
Loving so Understanding-Lord
Look at What – You-Have-Done
Look at what – You-Created
You-Gave-Me-Hell to Rule-For-you
I'll-Take-Heaven – For-My-Trouble

It-Is-Not – My-Fault
I-Just-Wanted to Live-My-Life
I-Would-Have – Been-Satisfied
With a Normal-Afterlife
Oh-God – Thank-You so Much
For-Making-Me – The-New-One and Only

(Chorus)
I Was Made By God
To Become Purgatory's Chosen One
By Killing Everyone And Sending Them To Hell
I Fell In Love Twice – I Was Betrayed And Killed
God Laughed As I Was Erased From Purgatory
And Sent To Hell To Take It Over For Him
After Ripping Off The Head Of Satan
82

Lyrical Stories Melody: Pages 83-98

The Gemini One Suite Trilogy: Songs 798-800
The Way I Was (798.)
A New Beginning (799.)
My End (The End #2) (800.)

Live Free For The Day – Live Free 'Til You Die
(In 11 Parts) (867.)
You Are The Answer / The World Awaits You
Take A Break / Don't Fall In Love / Save A Lady
Bullets In The Night Blood / Wash It Away / Ride On
Dying On The Road / Heads Or Tails

My Life Is Not So Great
(In 8 Parts) (882.)
Busted / Jail Time / Stabbed In The Back
Eating The Wall / I'm Nervous / I'm Out Of Here
Freedom / Busted Again

The Gemini One Suite Trilogy: Songs 798-800

The Way I Was (798.)

So-High – So-Down
Everyday is The-Same-Thing
One-That-I-Love is So-Fine
Why-Does-She – Stay-With-Me

Lazy – Hurts to Get-Up – Hurts to Walk
Sitting on The-Couch – Scratching-Myself is Easier
Stay-Inside – Sun and People – Are-Outside
Try-My-Best – Not to Be an Ass – When-She-Wakes-Me

(Chorus)
The Way I Was – The Way I Was
Was Like Nothing At All
With A Mind That Was Dying – Slowly
Time Ticked Away And I Did Not Care
Then One Night A Thought – Started My End

How-Am-I-Doing – I-Ask-Myself so Many-Times
Think-Hard – Then-I-Forget – Every-Time
What a Waste – My-Life-Is – Then-Again-What-Life
God – The-World – Won't-Help-Me – Lost-I'm-Lost
There is Another – New-Song – Playing-Inside-My-Mind

I'm-Tainted – I-Don't-Smile – I-Must-Go-Away
Start-With **#1** – Hide the Part of Myself
That-I-Don't-Like – That-I-Don't-Need – Any-More
Changing – Hurts-My-Mind – Can't-Stop-Now
Starting to Feel – Like a Person – With a New-Mind
Is-This the New-Me or Is-This-Something-Else

(Chorus)
The Way I Was – The Way I Was
Was Like Nothing At All
With A Mind That Was Dying – Slowly
Time Ticked Away And I Did Not Care
Then One Night A Thought – Started My End

A New Beginning (799.)

Song-After-Song – Speeds-Through-My-Mind
#67 – Who-Am-I – Slows-Me-Down
Mental-Block – Leads to Knowing
Way-Too-Much – For a Mind – That is Not-Ready
Sickness-Enters – My-Body – Sickness-Enters – My-Mind

(Chorus #1)
This Is A New Beginning
I Don't Have To Be Just Myself Anymore
We Is Empty – Feed We – Smiles And Frowns
We Is Empty – Feed We – Love And Hate

What is This – Feel so Nasty – Calmness-Comes-Slowly
Have to Slow-Down the Other – Voices in My-Mind
Back and Forth – Write-Two at the Same-Time
Voices – Sing their Songs while I'm-Creating
Mind is Too-Strong-Now – Won't let Me-Sleep
Who am I – Confusion – Clarity – We is Created

(Chorus #2)
This Is A New Beginning
I Don't Have To Be Just Myself Anymore
We Has Become – My Unreality To The Max
Now I Am A I – Who Can Think As A We

Everything is Great – I-Feel so Alive
Sky is Clear – Silence – Something is Wrong
Body – My-Body is Attacking-Me – With-No-Remorse
Doctors – Pills and Waiting – I'm-Okay-Again – Just-Like-That
What-Happened – I-Do-Not-Know – Changes is The-New-Me
Can-I – Finally-Become-New – Without-The-Pain – This-Time

(Chorus #1 & #2)
This Is A New Beginning
I Don't Have To Be Just Myself Anymore
We Is Empty – Feed We – Smiles And Frowns
We Is Empty – Feed We – Love And Hate
This Is A New Beginning For Me
I Don't Have To Be Just Myself Anymore
We Has Become – My Unreality To The Max
Now I Am A I – Who Can Think As A We

85

My End (The End #2) (800.)

Last-Days of My-Life – Brought-Change
Sickness – I-Died-Half-Way
Paused and Waiting – Here-We-Comes
From-The-Forever – Pool of Thoughts
Giving-Me-Back – Full-Life – Giving-Myself
Something-That-Smiles or Something-That-Bleeds

Out of Dreamworld – They-Came – Entities
Looking-For a Host – With-Half a Mind – Leftover
Found-One – That-Was-Sick and Erasing – Leftovers
New-Kind of Mind – Mixed with Aliens =
Dreams-Become-Reality – Reality a Nightmare
New-Kind of Mind – Feels a Presence
New-Kind of Mind – Has-Facts but No-Emotions
New-Kind of Mind – Starts-Singing a Song

(Chorus)
My End Has Come To Me
I'm Dead Inside Again
Being Who I Was Before
Makes Me Feel Nothing Inside
As I Watch My End Take We Away

Aliens-That-Eat-Dreams – Feel a Presence
Aliens-That-Eat-Dreams – Feel-Intoxicated
Dreams-That-Once – Were-Dreams – Are-Now-Different
Reality-Awaken – Reality-Are-Now- Dreams to Eat
Aliens-That-Eat-Dreams – Did-Not-Notice – Did-Not-Care
First-Time so Much – Dreams at One-Time
Causes-Guards to Go-Down – Succumbing to Reality

Mind-Rockin' – Created-With-The-Help of Aliens
Aliens-Addicted to Reality – Become-Trapped
New-Kind of Mind – Starts to Age – Ten-Times-Faster
New-Kind of Mind – Has to Release – Its-Mental-Prisoners

(Chorus)
My End Has Come To Me
I'm Dead Inside Again
Being Who I Was Before
Makes Me Feel Nothing Inside
As I Watch My End Take We Away

Live Free For The Day – Live Free 'Til You Die
(In 11 Parts) (867.)
You Are The Answer / The World Awaits You / Take A Break
Don't Fall In Love / Save A Lady / Bullets In The Night
Blood / Wash It Away / Ride On / Dying On The Road
Heads Or Tails

I. You Are The Answer

What is Perfect – In-This-World
I-Know-The-Answer – How-About-You
Why-The-Pause – Are-You-Stumped
Sweet-Mother-Earth – That is Such a Shame

I-Guess – It's-The-World's-Fault
That-The-Answer is Not-Quick
In-Your-Mind and Out of Your-Lips
Quite-Please – Here is The-Answer

(Chorus)
You Are The Answer
If You Do Not Kill
You Are The Answer
If You Do Not Rape
You Are The Answer
You Are A Great Person
The World Needs
More Persons Just Like You
(Repeat Chorus)

II. The World Awaits You

Wake-Up-Stranger
Time to Hit – The-Road
Ha-Ha – You're-Not-Alone
Are-You-Going to Wake-Her
Or-Slip-Away – With-No-Goodbye

Damn-That's-Hard and Understandable
What-Are-You – Going to Do
Take-Her – With-You
That's – Right – Stranger
Freedom is Calling-Out to You

(Chorus)
You Are Young – You Are Free
The World Awaits You
You Have Only One Life To Live
The World Awaits You
Enjoy Yourself Before You Get Old
The World Awaits You
Live Free For The Day
Live Free 'Til You Die
(Repeat Chorus)

III. Take A Break

The-Road is Long
The-Road is Hard
So-Many – Good-People
Never-Enough-Time
So-Many – Bad-People
Stoppers of Life and Fun

It's-Time – For-You to Rest – For a While
Have-Some-Alone-Time
Look at The-Moon and Stars
Remembering-Why – You-Are-Doing-This

(Chorus)
Take A Break – Take A Break Man
You Really Need It
Take A Break – Take A Break Man
Don't Let The Road
Bring You Down To The Ground
Take A Break – Take A Break Man
Why Not Drink A Beer
Why Not Get Laid

Take A Break – Take A Break Man
You Have Only One Life To Live
Take A Break – Take A Break Man
Live-Free – For-The-Day
Take A Break – Take A Break Man
Live-Free – 'Til-You-Die

(Repeat Chorus)

IV. Don't Fall In Love

Man O' Man
Did-You-Stay too Long
Your – Take a Break
Turned-Into a Stay – For-Awhile
While-You-Contemplated – Falling in Love

The-Road is Your-Life
The-Road is Your-Bride
Come on Man – Snap-Out of It

(Chorus)
Don't Fall In Love
It Will Make You Give Up The Road
Don't Fall In Love
That's What Everybody Does
Don't Fall In Love
You Can Get Laid Down The Road
Don't Fall In Love
Live Free For The Day
Live Free 'Til You Die

Love – How-Many-Times
Do-You-Want-Me to Say-Love
Okay-Man – One-More-Time
Love – That's-It
Now-Get-Back on Your-Bike and Ride
Time to Dust – Your-Ass-Off
Time to Make – Another-Dozen-Women
Purr and Moan – Like-Beautiful-Ladies

(Chorus)
Don't Fall In Love
It Will Make You Give Up The Road
Don't Fall In Love
That's What Everybody Does
Don't Fall In Love
You Can Get Laid Down The Road
Don't Fall In Love
Live Free For The Day
Live Free 'Til You Die

V. Save A Lady

She's on The-Run
From-Her – Crazy-Old-Man
She-Runs – Out in The-Road
Right in Front of Your-Path

Rubber-From – Your-Two-Wheels
Quick-Turn of The-Handle-Bars
She-Safe and Wanting a Ride
Down-This-Long and Lonely-Road

(Chorus)
Save A Lady
She'll Be Very Grateful
Save A Lady
Maybe She'll Let You Have Her
Save A Lady
Then Drop Her Off Down The Road
Before She Starts Getting Old
Thinking That She's Your Lady
(Repeat Chorus)

VI. Bullets In The Night

Come-On-Baby – Get-On
I'll-Give-You a Ride
That's it Baby – Hold on Tight
I'm a Speed-Demon
That-Owns – The-Road

Never-Mind is My-Name
What's-Your-Problem – Where-You-Heading
What-Was-That – You-Okay-Baby

(Chorus)
Bullets In The Night
Shoot Her in Her Back
Bullets In The Night
Shot-Out By Her Crazy Old Man
Bullets In The Night – Takes Her Life
As You Ride Like Hell To Save Yours
(Repeat Chorus)
90

VII. Blood

Gotta-Stop – Gotta-Stop-Riding-Man
Shooting-Madman is Miles-Behind-You
You're-Safe – You're-Safe – Slow-Down
Before-You-Crash to Your-Death

Control-Your-Rage – Find-Your-Center
Make-Your-Mind – Work-For-You
There-Was-Nothing – You-Could-Do

She is Dead – Killed-By a Monster
You're-Alive and Breathing
It's-Not-Your-Fault – That-Her-Blood
Has-Dried-Dark-Red – On-Your-Bike

(Chorus)
Blood Is Life – Blood Is Death
Blood Is Heaven – Blood Is Hell
It Is What It Is
Nothing Can Change That
Blood Is Life – Blood Is Death
Blood Is Heaven – Blood Is Hell
It Is What It Is
Nothing Can Change That
(Repeat Chorus)

VIII. Wash It Away

Hose-Splashing – Out a Stream
Hand-That is Holding-It – Is-Shaking
Blood-Flows – From-Your-Bike – Onto the Ground
Look-Out-For-Yourself – They'll-Never – Believe-You
It's-Not-Your-Fault – It's-The-Worlds
That-Condemns – The-Innocent and Frees-The-Guilty

(Chorus)
Wash It Away – Wash It All Away
Remember These Bloodstains
Wash It Away – Wash It All Away
Remember The World Can Kill You
Wash It Away – Wash It All Away – Then-Ride-On
(Repeat Chorus)
91

IX. Ride On

Live-Free – For-The-Day
Live-Free – 'Til-You-Die
Ride-On-Man – Ride-On
Get the Freaking – Hell-Out of There
One-Hundred – Miles-More
Will-Lift – Your-Road-Curse
You'll be Free – You'll be Free

Thunder-In – The-Night-Sky
Lightning-Strikes a Mountaintop
Rain – Clear-Cold-Rain
Soaks-Your-Tired and Withered-Body
One-Hundred – Miles-More
Will-Lift – Your-Road-Curse
You'll be Free – You'll be Free

(Chorus)
Ride On – Ride On
Beat Your Road Curse
Ride On – Ride On
You Own The Road
Ride On – Ride On
Only Death Can Stop You
From Saving Your Own Life

Don't-Close – Your-Eyes
Wake-Up – Wake-Up
Save – Your-Own-Life
Don't-Give-Up – Don't-Give-Up
Save-Your – Own-Life

Open-Your-Eyes – See-The-Lights of The-Truck
That is Going to Take – Your-Life – By-My-Design

(Chorus)
Ride On – Ride On
Beat Your Road Curse
Ride On – Ride On
You Own The Road
Ride On – Ride On
Only Death Can Stop You
From Saving Your Own Life

92

X. Dying On The Road

Bam – Crunch – Boom

Where-Did-That – Truck-Come-From
Closed-Eyes – Cannot-See
Death-Coming – Their-Way
Where-Did-That – Truck-Come-From
Closed-Eyes – Cannot-See
Death-Coming – Their-Way

(Chorus)
Your Life Flashes In Front Of You
As You Lie Dying On The Road
Your Journey Is Not Over Yet
As You Lie Dying On The Road
Will Your Soul Rise Or Will It Fall
As You Lie Dying On The Road
(Repeat Chorus)

XI. Heads Or Tails

Pray-All-You-Want – Your-Life is Over
Is-This-Fair – Is-This-Right – I-Don't-Care
Come-On-Man – Hurry-Up and Die
Why-Are-You – Holding-On – End-Your-Pain

I'm-Here-In-Hell – Waiting-For-Your-Soul
Remember-My-Words – I-Whispered – In-Your-Ears
Live-Free-For-The-Day – Live-Free-'Til-You-Die
Now-Close-Your-Eyes – And-Say-Goodbye

(Chorus)
Heads Or Tails
Like You Had A Choice
Heads Or Tails
Heaven – You Never Had A Chance
Heads Or Tails
Hell – Is Where You Soul Will Burn
Heads Or Tails
Hello – My Name Is Satan
And Yes I Have A Tail
(Repeat Chorus)
93

My Life Is Not So Great (In 8 Parts) (882.)
Busted / Jail Time / Stabbed In The Back / Eating The Wall /
I'm Nervous / I'm Out Of Here / Freedom / Busted Again

I. Busted

Walk-The-Streets – Hello-Victims
Just-Relax – This-Will be Almost
Painless – Long as You – Stay-Put
While-I-Run-Away – With-All-Your-Money

Excuse-The-Knock – On-Your-Head
Not-Deadly – Just-Forceful
I-Have to Make-Sure – You-Understand
The-Pain and The-Sorrow of My-Life
Gives-Me-No-Choice – I-Have to Survive

(Chorus)
Busted – I'm Busted
Damn The Man
Why Can't They Leave Me Alone
Busted – I'm Busted
Because I Have No Money
Because I Have To Find Some
Is It My Fault – That It Belongs
To Somebody Else Before I Get It

(Repeat Chorus)

II. Jail Time

I-Had-The-Right to Remain-Silent
I-Had-My-Day – In-Court
I-Had-The-Right to Speak
No-One-Listened or Cared
Guilty – On-All-Accounts

I-Have-Ten-Years – And a Day to Go
Man in The-Next-Cell – Likes to Kill
He's-Serving-Five – For-Murder
He-Was-Smart – He-Took-No-Money
Just-Three-Lives – With a Knife

94

(Chorus)
Jail Time Is Not Fun Time
Jail Time Sucks To Hell
Jail Time Is Not For Me
No Way Can I Go On Like This
Either I Bust Out – Or I'll Die Trying
(Repeat Chorus)

III. Stabbed In The Back

Do-My-Job – Stay-Out of The-Way
Don't-Want – Don't-Need to Die
Before-I-Taste and Feel-Freedom

I'm-In – My-Own-World
Never-Do-I-See – Never-Do-I-Hear
Men-Cry – Bleed-Or-Die

(Chorus)
Watching My Front
While I Was Getting
Stabbed In The Back
All I Want To Do Is Escape
Now I'm Going To Bleed To Death
On The Floor – From Being
Stabbed In The Back

Locked-Up and Surviving
Until-I-Came – Around a Corner
Stepping-In a Pool of Blood

Eyes-Made-Contact – Voices of Warning
My-Days – Are-Numbered – I'm-Dead
I'm-Not-In – My-Own-World – Anymore

(Chorus)
Watching My Front
While I Was Getting
Stabbed In The Back
All I Want To Do Is Escape
Now I'm Going To Bleed To Death
On The Floor – From Being
Stabbed In The Back

IV. Eating The Wall

I'm-Not-Insane – They-Tried to Kill-Me
I'm-Not-Insane – Soaking-In – My-Own-Blood
Madhouse – I-Will-Make – My-New-Home
I'm-Not-Insane – I'm-Totally-Sane
When-I-Start – Eating-The-Wall

(Chorus)
Hey Look At Me – I'm Eating The Wall
It Taste So Very Good – Needs Some Salt
Hey Look At Me – I'm Eating The Wall
Would You Like Some – It Needs Some Salt

(Repeat Chorus)

V. I'm Nervous

Spiders-On-My-Face – Licking-My-Saliva
My-Pills – No-Calm – Just-My-Mind-Tripping
While-I-Gnaw – On-My-Arm-Restraints
Almost-There – I-Have to Keep-Laughing
Make-Them-Believe – I'm-Crazy

(Pre-Chorus)
Face In The Mirror – I Can Not Help You
I'm Lost In A World – That Can Not Be For Real

(Chorus)
I'm Nervous – I'm Nervous About Everything
Being Sane And Stable In Here
Will Get You Tied Up And Gagged
I'm Nervous – I'm Nervous About Everything
Can't Seem To Remember
What I Did – To Be Stuck In Here

Pills – My-Pills – That-Calm-Me
I-Hate-Them – They-Are so Dirty
When-They – Saturate-My-Clean-Mind
Making – Me-Feel so Strange
Like a Happy-Clown – In a Horror-Movie

(Repeat Pre-Chorus & Chorus)

VI. I'm Out Of Here

I'm – Getting-Better
Tonight-I-Sleep – Without-Restraints
I'm – Getting-Better
Very-Soon – I'll-Make-My-Escape

I'm – Getting-Better
My-Mind is Almost – Fully-Back
I'm – Getting-Better
My-Pills – That-Calm-Me – I-Hate-Them
Found a Way to Toss-Them-Away

(Chorus)
I'm Out Of Here
Ain't Never Coming Back
I'm Out Of Here
I'm Not Crazy – I'm A Victim
I'm Out Of Here
No One Better Get In My Way
I'm Out Of Here – I'm Out Of Here
The World Can Kiss My Sane Ass

Have to Get-Out of This-Place
Food-Tastes – Like-Glue – Mixed-With-Dirt
Have to Get-Out of This-Place
Tired of Talking to Only-Crazy-People

Have to Get-Out of This-Place
Make-Friendly – With-The-Ugly-Nurse
Take-Her-Keys and Lock-Her in The-Closet
Have to Get-Out of This-Place
Before – I – Go – Crazy

(Chorus)
I'm Out Of Here
Ain't Never Coming Back
I'm Out Of Here
I'm Not Crazy – I'm A Victim
I'm Out Of Here
No One Better Get In My Way
I'm Out Of Here – I'm Out Of Here
The World Can Kiss My Sane Ass

VII. Freedom

Lonely-Ugly-Nurse
Looking-For-Love – In a Madhouse
Lonely-Ugly-Nurse
Fell-In-Love – With-Someone-Sane
Lonely-Ugly-Nurse
Thought-I-Was-Crazy – Like-I-Care

Escaped – Over-The-Wall
Freedom is My-Prize
Escaped – Over-The-Wall
While-Every-Body – Was in Bed – Drugged and Sleeping

(Chorus)
Freedom – I Have It
About Damn Time
Freedom – I Have It
That's What They Get
For Thinking That I'm Crazy
(Repeat Chorus)

VIII. Busted Again

Alive and Free – Wanting to Be-Obscene
While a Pretty-Lady – Is-Talking to Me
We're-In a Groove – When-Blue-Lights-Flash
Screech of Tires – Guns-Pulled-Out – Men-In-Blue
Won't-Even-Let-Me – Have-Five-Minutes

(Chorus)
Busted – I'm Busted Again
Damn The Man
Why Can't They Leave Me Alone
Busted – I'm Busted Again
Where Do I Go From Here
Back To The Madhouse – Or – Back To The State-Pen

Should-I-Run – Freedom or Death
Everything is So-Loud – Hard to Hear
Roar-Leads to Sudden-Silence – My-Mind-Clears
Death is Final – Life – Always-Another-Chance
(Repeat Chorus)
98

Short Story #2: Space-Sex = Space Clap
(Pages 99-103)

John a janitor at Mars Station Number Eight is not enjoying a cup of cold bitter coffee. His life sucks bad. He was kicked off of Earth with a punishment of ten years on Mars.

Working hard for no pay all day, then at night John is allowed the privilege of staying in a sterilized room all by himself 'til first morning's light . His crime. Getting drunk, getting high and having sex with both of the Mayor's young but legal daughters at the same time without asking the Mayor's permission first.

John feels deeply that he got a very bad rap, especially since neither of the Mayor's daughters were that great of a lay. Escape is no way ever. What can one like John do, run outside to freedom where there is no oxygen to breathe?

Every day is the same, John has lost count as to how many years he has be stuck and forgotten about on Mars. (It has only been three and a half years.)

John is stir crazy and horny as Hell. When he whacks off only the memories in his lonely mind of the ladies he has had sex with in the past are there to turn him on. Sadly even these memories are beginning to fade away to almost forgotten.

Fortunately for John things are about to change for him, for tomorrow he will have the chance to steal one of the very same space ships that brought him, and everyone else to Mars, to be a cast away prisoner.

Let's move forward to where John is flying his stolen space ship, his destination is the outer reaches of space, a sad attempt as he dreams of a far away planet where there is no one in the waiting for him to bring him back to Mars.

John can easily fly this type of space ship. However for some reason this ship has been fitted with advanced technology that he is unfamiliar with.

John scratches his head and his ass but neither of them are doing him any good. He yells at himself to hurry up and make a decision, as four ships are creeping up on him from behind. Sweat appears on his forehead as he watches the monitor knowing that if he does not do something very fast he will be captured and punished for escaping.

John cannot wait anymore and pushes a blue button. The space ship almost feels like it comes to a pause as it begins to start to shake from gathering up an unbelievable amount of power.

John is screaming out loud, 'Oh Shit!' As his stolen and only one of its class space ship takes off with a speed Mankind has not traveled before.

John, who is not at this time thinking about getting laid, is scared shitless without a trace of a smile on his lips. He's in a panic as he screams out, 'What the fuck did I just do?'

No answer, only pain caused by miles passing by faster than the speed of light. Flip the blue switch that lies under the blue button John is telling himself and his body can barely comply.   It takes him a little under ten minutes to flip the blue switch that allows this space ship to return to a nice safe speed of space traveling.

John, in slight shock from speeding so very inhumanly, looks around and cannot believe what his blue human eyes see to be for real. Space ships, so many different types flying around like cars driving on a highway, on any highway on Earth.

John now notices that his ship has stalled as a smaller ship than his goes flying by him with a pilot that seems to be giving him his middle finger. He restarts his ship saying out loud, 'Fuck you exists strongly through out the universe.'

John is not sure of the driving laws for this space ship highway that appears to lead to a space station. He takes his ship onward until his ship is one among hundreds of ships on this highway.

John has to come to a stop so he parks his ship and looks over at the lane next to his. What he sees almost makes him jump out of his seat. There are two hot looking alien ladies waving at him wearing hardly anything at all.

John says to them, "Please fuck me," but of course they cannot hear him. Then out of John's ship communication console comes the strange alien ladies' language. John does what he must and starts talking Earthling to these two alien ladies as hot and as sexy as his going out of sexual control mind allows him to do.

To John's surprise these two ladies start laughing and shaking their heads at him, just like two Earth ladies would do if they were still interested in him, but now know that they have him wrapped around their alien lady fingers.

They are now pointing at the front of John's space ship like they want him to allow them to pull in front of him and then for him to follow them to the greatest sexual experience of his human life. John says yes to himself, then he blows these two hot alien ladies a kiss and gives then a double thumbs up for good measure.

Traffic sucks in space just like it does on Earth because it takes John over an hour to finally park his space ship and introduce himself all horny, gentleman like to his two future sexual alien lady sex partners.

Moments later they are walking to a hotel to get a room. John has had sex with an Earth lady that spoke a different language and it made little difference when love or sex was what's on your mind.

This John thinks to himself as he watches two (yes count them twice for John is about to two times enjoy and feel sex or fucking like no man on Earth has ever done before) sexy and built alien ladies take off their clothes. What is even hotter is all they are wearing are dresses with nothing but naked alien lady parts underneath them.

Two naked, and almost Earth looking, female alien ladies speak their sexy sounding language as one to John, as they walk over to him to caress and undress him.

A few kisses and touch moments later John stands naked and hung, being stared at by two alien ladies who look like they just hit the big pecker jackpot. He is just about to go in for a longer contact moment, when his two mystery, alien ladies begin to hiss making he take a step back when they pounce on him.

The first hot sexy blueish and greenish alien lady lands naked, crotch on John's face knocking him to the floor.

The second hot alien lady, that is very close in color to her friend but also has the color red added to her skin tone quickly jumps on top of John's crotch.

John freaks out at first and almost tosses alien lady #1 off his face until he feels that unforgettable feeling that he has not felt in so very long on his pecker.

John is in the moment of pleasing one as another pleases him as alien lady #1 removes herself from his face and leans down to him so they are face to face. He looks into her double set of eyes as she quickly sticks a needle into the right side of his neck.

John cannot move and feels like he is going to pass out as alien lady #2 stops riding him so alien lady #1 can have her turn on top of his Earth pecker. Life still sucks for John, for he passed out before he felt himself finish.

The act was done and over with when John awoke the next morning naked and all by himself. John says, 'Welcome to space fucking 101,' to himself as he walks to the bathroom to take a piss.

1-2-3-4-5-6-7-8-9-10. 'Ouch! Ouch! Ouch!"

John is screaming as he is looking at his pecker that is burning like it is on fire and is now the same colors of the two alien ladies that drugged him the night before.

John gets dressed and walks to where his ship is parked and realizes harshly that he was rolled like a mark. He looks around and wishes to himself that he was back on Mars in his sanitized room all safe with a pecker that looks like it comes from Earth, instead of outer space. Three days later John dies all alone and painfully from a very severe case of space clap.

1:49 pm, August 29, 2019. A lot has happened since this book was first published on August 16, 2016. To go along with The Gemini Rising Rockin' Machine, I created Keith Starblue. Which is my second author's name and has nothing to do at all with Mind Rockin. Since the spring of 2016, until July twelfth 2019, I have written eighteen books as Keith Starblue, (Nine Novels & nine books of short stories.) I am happy and proud that I have written six books this year of 2019 and I have already started on another novel. After this novel is finished I'm going to start writing on my tenth book of short stories. This will make it that I have written twenty books in three and a half years. It's hard to believe looking back that I have passed up my goal of writing four books a year and I'm truly delighted as Hell that I did.

It's hard to believe that one night back in 2005, while I was drunk and high, I planted the roots of what would grow to become Mind Rockin. I went into my closet and pulled out some boxes to find something. (Which I cannot even remember what I was looking for now.) I stacked a box on top of another box and they were too close behind me so I knocked them over while backing up away from the closet.

It was the bottom box that contained my future. Which was a folder of a few songs that I wrote the lyrics to. About forty or so. Some of these songs dated back to the late 80's. Twice in my life a shoe box with songs that I wrote the lyrics to got thrown away upon moving and the third time I burned the third box of songs one night after reflecting how fucked up my life was at that time. If I would have never knocked a box over and spilled its contents out on the floor, I would have never created Mind Rockin'. Thus I would have never created Keith Starblue or my third author's name, Gemini Starblue. Which I'm going to release on the world in 2020. And sooner than later I will release my final Mind Rockin' book – Fuckaholic: The Book of Bad Songs. Until then, Mind Rock On.

The soon to be deceased, Gemini Rising Rockin' Machine.

www.ingramcontent.com/pod-product-compliance
Lightning Source LLC
Chambersburg PA
CBHW070504130626
46555CB00003B/1158